**“Nice to meet you, Zoey.”**

“You, too.” Zoey watched her neighbor and new colleague walk down the path. She moved with surety and confidence, and very briefly Zoey felt envious of her. Erin seemed to be a woman who knew who she was, who had found her place in the world and was very comfortable there, whereas Zoey felt like she was back at the beginning. Forging a new path in life, uncertain of where it would lead or who she even was! She’d spent so long pleasing others and fitting into everyone’s expectations of her that she’d lost who she used to be, and she hoped that by moving here, she would rediscover just who had been hiding all these years beneath layers of dutiful domesticity.

Maybe one day she would be like Erin? Her *own* version, anyway. And maybe Monday wouldn’t be so scary now? Because she already knew someone. Someone whom she could feel safe with?

*Let’s hope we really do get on.*

*Because I’ve got to live right next door to her if I don’t!*

Dear Reader,

I wanted to do something special for my fortieth medical romance with Harlequin and I'd always wanted to tell the story of two female doctors finding one another in a small seaside town, and so Dr. Zoey Marsh and Dr. Erin Bramble came to life on the page!

I love Zoey for her heart and her bravery. So many women in life have made themselves small to fit into a mold that other people expect, and I wanted to give Zoey a chance to break that mold. And Erin is the one who was courageous from the start, not afraid to say what she wanted from life, having the desire to reach out and claim it, only to lose it all through no fault of her own.

What if, I thought, these two women met? Both so cruelly hurt, but finding a comfort and love in the other that mends the broken pieces of their hearts?

So I gave Erin and Zoey Westcombe Bay.

And I gave them each other.

I hope you enjoy their story!

Happy reading!

*Louisa* xxx

# GP'S FRESH START SUMMER

LOUISA HEATON

MEDICAL ROMANCE

Recycling programs for this product may not exist in your area.

ISBN-13: 978-1-335-95287-5

GP's Fresh Start Summer



For questions and comments about the quality of this book, please contact us at CustomerService@Harlequin.com.

Harlequin Enterprises ULC
22 Adelaide St. West, 41st Floor
Toronto, Ontario M5H 4E3, Canada
www.Harlequin.com

HarperCollins Publishers
Macken House, 39/40 Mayor Street Upper,
Dublin 1, D01 C9W8, Ireland
www.HarperCollins.com

**Printed in U.S.A.**

1 2 3 4 5 6 7 8 9 10 HDC 29 28 27 26

**Louisa Heaton** lives on Hayling Island, Hampshire, with her husband, four children and a small zoo. She has worked in various roles in the health industry—most recently four years as a community first responder, answering emergency calls. When not writing, Louisa enjoys other creative pursuits, including reading, quilting and patchwork—usually instead of the things she *ought* to be doing!

**Books by Louisa Heaton**

**Harlequin Medical Romance**

***Christmas North and South***

*A Mistletoe Marriage Reunion*

***Cotswold Docs***

*Best Friend to Husband?*
*Finding a Family Next Door*

***Royal York Hospital***

*New Year to Nine-Month Surprise*

*Single Mom's Alaskan Adventure*
*Finding Forever with the Firefighter*
*Resisting the Single Dad Surgeon*
*The Surgeon's Relationship Ruse*
*One Night to Twin Miracle*
*Nurse's Night Before Valentine's*
*Onboard and Off Limits*

Visit the Author Profile page
at Harlequin.com for more titles.

For Nick

# CHAPTER ONE

A WEDGE OF deep blue sea appeared in the valley of the two green hills as Dr Zoey Marsh drove towards her new home in the seaside village of Westcombe Bay. It glittered in the sun, and on the shimmering horizon she could see the dark grey blur of two ships. A container vessel and maybe something smaller. The sea air filled the car and now she was closer, the screech of seagulls could be heard overhead and she had to flip her visor down to shield her gaze from the scorching overhead sun.

She could feel herself growing lighter the closer she got. The weight of the last few years' turmoil lifting as she remembered childhood visits here. Riding on the donkeys on the beach. Fish and chips, dripping with salt and vinegar, on the seafront. Crabbing in the rockpools and nestling under blankets, exhausted at night after a full day playing, in the caravan opposite her younger sister, Hazel. They'd been good days. Innocent days. And she was glad that she was returning here, to start a new life after fifteen years of marriage and, most recently, two years of being a widow.

*I'm only thirty-seven. Plenty of life still left in me.*

The road swept down towards Westcombe. She passed caravan sites, camping sites and homes and cottages before she drove through Westcombe's busy High Street, passing shops and businesses. Being Saturday, the place was packed with shoppers and tourists. She saw a sign for the Westcombe Bay Medical Practice and peered down the lane to see if she could see it. She couldn't see anything before her sat-nav instructed her to turn left as she approached the harbour where all the fishing vessels were moored and the thick smell of fish and brine came through her open window. The new road took her past the harbour and along the crescent sweep of the bay, with its lovely sandy beach, dotted with families and couples stretched out on towels, their bodies gleaming with suncream. Then the road curved inwards slightly, past the crazy golf course and up onto the hill.

Leaning forward, she gazed at the cottages nestled against the slopes. One of those was hers. She'd come to view it a couple of months ago at her sister's urging, strolling through the empty rooms and gazing out of the windows at the stunning view she had over the bay and realising she would never find a better place. The two-bedroomed cottage was perfect. Not too big and with an extra bedroom if Hazel wanted to sleep over on occasion. That would be nice, the two of them together.

Not that it would only be two of them for long. Hazel was seven months pregnant from a one-night stand and had practically begged Zoey to come to Westcombe so that she didn't have to go through pregnancy and motherhood alone. And despite the fact that Zoey had wanted a fresh start, a new beginning in which she didn't have to keep putting other people's happiness first all the time, she'd come anyway. Because Westcombe held such happy memories and Zoey liked the idea of being close to a baby she could spoil and cuddle. She and Brad had never managed to have children in the fifteen years of their marriage and it had always been a source of sorrow for her. But not for the reasons most people would think. And she and Hazel were close. She loved her sister very much and because their parents had emigrated to Australia all those years ago, they were all the other had left to rely on. Especially if there were an emergency.

She turned right onto Mariner's Lane and drove about halfway along it, parking behind her removals lorry that had arrived here before her to her new home, Seaglass Cottage. The guys were sitting on the low brick wall in front of her property, T-shirts off, enjoying the sun, and she gave them a quick wave to show that she had the keys and would be out of her vehicle in a minute.

There was an element of disbelief still about what she was doing. She'd lived in Guildford for most of her life. As a child in Shackleford, she'd moved out to study at Southampton for her medical degree, where she'd impulsively married Brad and then returned to Guildford, to live in Merrow, as a wife and a GP.

She'd never stepped out of the lane expected of her after that. She had always done the dutiful thing. Had lived her life to a well set out timetable and never varied from it. Even Brad's family had expressed dismay that she was going to sell their home and move away.

*'But why, Zoey?'*

*'We'll never see you!'*

*'Don't you think you owe it to Brad's memory to stay?'*

*'You're so happy here. Why would you want to leave?'*

Well, they had no idea. She couldn't *breathe* there. Had felt stifled for far too long and the desire to just break out of the rut she'd been so very carefully manoeuvred into by Brad's family, had been strong.

It was *her* life she had to live. Not theirs. And so, with the desire to reconnect and help her sister, she'd applied for the GP posting at Westcombe Bay Medical Practice and looked for a property near Hazel. Hazel lived in a small flat above a shop near the library.

As she stepped out of her car, one of the removal guys met her, wiping his brow with his T-shirt, revealing a neat little six-pack beneath.

Zoey averted her gaze politely.

'Dr Marsh! Good morning. You made good time?'

She smiled at George and nodded. 'I did! The A3 was a bit clogged leaving Guildford, but once I was clear of it, it's been pretty plain sailing. Once we get inside, I can get you guys a drink as it's so hot.'

'That's kind. Thanks. They reckon up to thirty degrees today, so if it's all right with you, we'll get you unpacked as soon as. The lads reckon we can be done by lunch so we can steal an hour down on the beach before we go home.'

She smiled. 'Sounds perfect. I'll open up.' Zoey hurried up the front path, inserted the key and turned it, swinging the front door open wide. This place was *hers*. With time, it would become a home, but for now? She had to stand back and let the guys do their thing. She'd brought one box with her of kitchen things. The kettle, tea, milk, juice, spoons and mugs, and she fetched that from her car, weaving in between the men hefting boxes to various rooms. In the kitchen, she rolled up the blind at the window and looked out into the garden. It hadn't been shown any love lately, but it was small enough and manageable and she knew she would get to it at some point. There was a small patio area, a patch of grass and a couple of raised beds. Clematis and climbing roses ran along the fence at the back. There was also a small red-leafed acer.

Once she'd made the removals men a drink each, she unlocked the back door and pushed it open and stepped outside, sucking in a deep breath. She had so many hopes pinned on this place! This was her future. It had to go right! It had to, but it was so unnerving to be so far away from everything that she'd once known. Had her parents felt the same way when they'd arrived in Australia to live? Mum said it had been strange at first, but now they were thriving. Zoey could only hope that she would get to feel the same, because she'd spent the last two years *surviving*, not thriving. And maybe even before that, too.

'Hello, love. Just moving in, are you?' A face appeared at the garden boundary. A white-haired old man with a kind face. 'I'm Jack.'

One of her new neighbours!

'Hi. Zoey. And yes, moving in day.'

'Be nice to have someone next door again. Just these three cottages along here. Your place has been empty for months and the lady on the other side of you is a doctor, so I don't get to talk to her much.'

'She's a doctor? At Westcombe practice?'

Jack nodded. 'Keeps herself to herself.'

'I'll be working with her then.'

'You a nurse or something?'

'I'm a doctor, too. I start Monday.'

'Well, I'll be. Two doctors for neighbours! I guess you're the best ones to have in case my old ticker starts playing me up again.'

Zoey smiled. 'You live on your own, Jack?'

'Got my Betty with me.'

'Your wife?'

He laughed. 'My dog. She's twelve. We're having a competition to see who will outlive who.'

She liked Jack immensely. He had the same type of humour as her own father.

'What about you, love? You married? Got kids?'

'I'm on my own.' She didn't want to give her life story over a fence.

'So, I've got me a quiet neighbour, then?'

'Well, sometimes I've been known to sing whilst I'm gardening and this place looks like it needs a little bit of TLC, so I hope that's all right?' she said with a smile.

He nodded, smiled. 'Do you do song requests?'

Zoey laughed. 'If I know the words.'

'I like you, Zoey. Me and you will do fine. Well, I won't keep you. I'm sure you've got a lot to organise.'

'Nice to meet you, Jack.'

'You too, love. You too.'

A removals lorry had turned up outside. She'd heard its rumbling engine and the squeak of its air brakes and then the loud voices of the men as they'd got out and waited for the owner to turn up. Erin had groaned and pulled the pillow over her head to block out the noise as she'd only just got to bed after being on a callout from three this morning. Tom Pritchard had rung her private number at just after two thirty, panicking, frightened that Evie, his wife, was breathing funny. She'd given Tom her number weeks ago, after his wife had been diagnosed with metastatic bowel cancer, and told him that if he ever needed her, no matter what the time of night, he was to call. Because she'd grown to know Tom and Evie over the last year and Evie's diagnosis had been a shock, even if she had been unwell for some time.

There'd been so many *what ifs*. What if Evie had come in earlier? What if she hadn't dismissed so many of her symptoms? What if she'd not been embarrassed about the bleeding from her back passage? Then maybe this would have been different and Evie wouldn't have spent the last week bedbound, unwilling to eat or drink. Tom had managed to get some water down his wife, but not much, and when her phone had rung in the early hours, Erin had simply *known.* She'd dressed quickly, driven to their home and confirmed to Tom that Evie was in the process of dying. That he should sit with her and hold her hand. That Erin would make sure that Evie wasn't in any pain and would have dignity and love as she took her last breath, which she did just after five o'clock that morning.

She'd sat with them both and notified the funeral home, and the undertakers had arrived at about 8:30 a.m. to take Evie away. After that, she'd completed all the death paperwork, left Tom with his sister, who'd arrived, and then driven home herself to try and catch up on some much-needed sleep. She'd got maybe an hour and then the lorry had arrived. And now the owner was here, by the sound of things outside, and there was the noise of clanking metal and thuds and footsteps and laughter, when all she'd wanted to do was sleep.

Groaning, she'd swung her feet out of bed and headed downstairs for coffee. Her body ached and she felt low, but it was another beautiful day outside and so she stepped out into the garden to have her coffee on the patio, hoping the morning sunshine would lift her spirits after such a sad start.

She heard voices. Her neighbour, Jack, talking to the new owner, and though she knew it was the polite thing to stand up and wave hello, she chose not to. She wasn't ready yet, still needing to process the events of the night before. The loss of a patient. And besides, she had bedhead, probably had bags under her eyes and was in her llama pyjamas and who needed to see that first thing in the morning? She told herself she'd go and introduce herself later when she was feeling much more human and sociable. And she'd made that lemon and poppy seed cake yesterday evening at cooking class, so maybe she could take that round as a welcome gift? Maybe seeing someone smile and making a new friend would lift her out of the gloom that lingered, having watched a man lose the wife he'd loved for over forty years. She knew the pain of losing someone you loved. Of not having them in your life any more, and it was a difficult thing to process.

A couple of hours later, she'd showered, freshened up and noticed that the removals men were closing up their lorry and getting ready to go. The men clambered into the truck and were just driving off as Erin headed up her new next-door neighbour's garden path to knock on the door.

'Just a minute!' she heard someone call from inside. A woman's voice. And then the door was swung open wide and she saw a petite woman with white blonde hair and bright blue eyes. She was dressed in an oversize blue linen shirt and tight denim shorts, revealing legs that hadn't seen the sun for some time but were toned and perfect and ended in a pair of cute pink canvas shoes. 'Hi!' she said.

'Hi. I'm Erin, your next-door neighbour. Thought I'd better introduce myself.'

The woman beamed a genuine broad smile. 'Hello, Erin. I'm Zoey.' And she stuck out her hand for Erin to shake.

She shook, her brain scrambling to think of something to say and then it seemed to register that in her other hand she held a cling-film-wrapped offering. 'I…er…brought you this! It's lemon and poppy seed, I hope that's okay?' Erin felt as if she was waffling. She didn't normally waffle.

'Actually, it's one of my favourites! Did you bake it? It looks homemade.'

'I did. I go to a local cookery class on a Friday evening which, now I come to think of it, sounds really pathetic, like why don't I have something more exciting to do on a Friday evening, but…'

She trailed off, felt her cheeks flushing. She was still holding Zoey's hand! Erin released it and passed over the cake. 'Anyway. Enjoy.' She turned, desperate to get away, to get back to her own house and try to work out why her normally well-behaved brain had somehow managed to crumble into pieces and stop working.

'Wait! Would you like to come in for a slice? I could make tea, or something cold, if you'd prefer?'

Erin turned back around to say *No, thanks. I'm really busy, actually, but it was nice to meet you.*

'That'd be nice, thanks,' she said instead, and found herself stepping over the threshold of Seaglass Cottage and into a maze of boxes and bags and random items dotted here, there and everywhere.

'Sorry about the mess,' Zoey said after closing the front door, squeezing past her, her scent of fresh moss, blackcurrants and oriental spices wafting their way up Erin's nose, dizzying her senses.

'Oh, it's no problem. Don't worry about it,' she said, trailing the diminutive blonde into her kitchen. Erin liked the way she walked. The way her oversize shirt drifted over her body.

The kitchen was just as full of boxes. One in particular sat on a wooden table in the heart of the room, lid splayed open, a trail of bubble wrap dripping over the side where clearly Zoey had begun to unpack. It looked as if it contained plates and bowls and one or two mugs nestled into the corners. And was there anyone else here? Had she moved in alone?

'So...tea or something cold?'

*If I pick a cold drink, I can get out of here faster.* 'Something cold is fine.'

'Water? Juice?'

'Sounds great.' Erin smiled.

'Which one?'

She flushed again. 'Juice. Thanks.' She looked around her for something to say. Something that would take the focus off the fact that her brain was seemingly short-circuiting right now. 'Looks like you're going to be busy for a while. You doing this all by yourself?'

Zoey located two mugs, rinsed them out, dried them, then poured two measures of orange juice from the fridge. 'Yes. Mugs okay? I haven't found my glassware yet.'

'Oh, fine.' Alone. *Single.*

'It's juice with bits.' She passed Erin the mug.

'I love bits.'

*I love bits? Groan.*

Zoey gave her a good-natured smile, as if she was amused. 'Jack tells me you're a doctor at the Westcombe Medical Practice, is that right?'

*Ah, good. Safer ground.*

'Yes! I started there as a locum actually, and I've become a permanent member of staff there for the last year.' *Please don't disappoint me and ask about a mysterious rash you've had for ages.*

'And you like it there? It's a nice place to work?'

*No rash.*

'The best. There's something more intimate about working in a small village. You know everyone so much better, because your patient list isn't as big. What about you, Zoey, what do you do?'

She looked like she might be an artist of some kind. There was an easel leaning up against the far wall. Erin could imagine her standing barefoot in front of a canvas, her white blonde hair up in a scarf, one hand holding a palette with a mass of colours, maybe one or two hair tousles hanging down, a paintbrush wedged crossways in her mouth as she studied her subject. A smudge of paint on the tip of her button nose.

Zoey smiled at her. 'Well, actually, I'm going to be a doctor there, too! I start Monday,' she said, waiting for her reaction.

Her struggling brain seemed to grind to a halt and stalled. Keiko, the practice manager, had mentioned that they had a new doctor starting on Monday, a Dr Marsh from Guildford, but she'd never thought for one minute that she'd be moving in next door!

'*You're* Dr Marsh?'

'I am! Pleased to meet you!'

Erin smiled politely.

# CHAPTER TWO

HER NAME WAS Erin Bramley. *Dr* Erin Bramley, of course, and Zoey discovered that she, too, lived alone. Except for her cat, Pixie.

'She's totally deaf, so she's a house cat. For safety,' Erin added, swallowing the rest of her juice and emptying the glass.

'Can I get you another?' Zoey offered, reaching for her glass.

'Oh! No, that's fine. I'm probably already encroaching on your time. You have a lot to do,' she said, getting to her feet and checking her pockets to remember which one held her keys.

Zoey thought her very stylish. The kind of style that she'd often wished she possessed. Some people had it, others didn't, and Zoey was most definitely one of the others. Though that might have something to do with the fact that Zoey went for comfort over style *every time*. Here they were, Saturday lunchtime, and Erin was wearing the kind of clothes that Zoey would consider for a job interview. Fitted black linen trousers, a floaty cream blouse. Erin's honey blonde hair was up in a clip but her long fringe hung loose and effortlessly perfect.

'You don't want a slice of cake?'

Erin seemed to think about it. 'No, thanks. I'm…er…meeting someone for lunch and don't want to spoil my appetite.'

'Oh, okay. More for me, then!' She walked Erin to the door, glad that she had called around. It meant that she had met both of her neighbours today and they both seemed lovely, which was great. 'I guess I'll see you on Monday.'

Erin nodded and smiled. 'Nice to meet you, Zoey.'

'You too.' Zoey watched her neighbour and colleague walk down the path. She moved with a surety and confidence and very briefly Zoey felt envious of her. Erin seemed to be a woman who knew who she was. Who had found her place in the world and was very comfortable there, whereas Zoey felt as if she was back at the beginning. Forging a new path in life, uncertain of where it would lead or who she even was! She'd spent so long pleasing others and fitting into everyone's expectations of her that she'd lost who she used to be, and she hoped that by moving here she would rediscover just who had been hiding all these years beneath layers of dutiful domesticity.

Maybe one day she would be like Erin. Her *own* version, anyway. And maybe Monday wouldn't be so scary now. Because she already knew someone. Someone with whom she could feel safe.

*Let's hope we really do get on.*

*Because I've got to live right next door to her if I don't!*

She was just about to close her door and return to her unpacking and maybe a slice of that delicious-looking cake that her neighbour had made when Erin suddenly turned around at Zoey's gatepost. 'Zoey?'

She felt her heart lift. 'Yes?'

'Would you like to join me for supper? I just figured that until you unpack fully, you were probably just going to grab takeaway or something and wondered if you'd like to do that together?'

Wow! What a lovely gesture. And she was right. She had thought about driving down into Westcombe and grabbing some fish and chips. Something that she hadn't had in *years.*

'That'd be great!'

'About sixish?'

Zoey beamed. 'Sounds perfect. I'll look forward to it. Thanks!'

'You're welcome. See you later.'

'You will.' Zoey closed her door, unable to

stop smiling the most genuine smile she'd felt in years. She felt light and free. Accepting an invitation to something spontaneous and making a new friend. Honestly?

When she'd spotted Erin at her door earlier, the woman had scared her to death! She'd looked so well put together it made Zoey feel drab in comparison. A pigeon next to a swan. She was so beautiful that having her sit in Zoey's kitchen, knowing that the woman was observing her whilst she bustled about making drinks and chatting about God only knew what, had unnerved her. And so she'd babbled, trying not to notice the way the sun coming in through the window warmed Erin's soft-looking skin. Tried not to notice the elegant way Erin's hands sat in her lap or held the glass of juice. And she'd tried so hard to calm her thundering heart and act normal. Honestly, the way Erin had got up and left so quickly, Zoey had wondered if she'd scared her new neighbour away!

But obviously not.

*Tonight, I'll try to be a bit calmer. Just be myself.*

'Oh, what will I wear?' she said out loud, staring at all the boxes and wondering if she had any nice clothes she could fish out of her suitcase. What was the expected attire for going out for a takeaway with a female friend? Smart casual?

Or just casual? She didn't want to look like she hadn't made an effort and neither did she want to look like she'd tried too hard! So she resorted to an old habit when she couldn't solve a problem.

Distraction.

Zoey reached into her shorts back pocket and pulled out her phone and dialled her sister's number. 'Hey, I've arrived! I'm here!'

'That's brilliant! You made good time, then?'

'I did.'

'Are the removals guys still there? Any hunky young studs with six-packs that might be interested in a woman who is heavily pregnant and hasn't washed her hair and has spent half the morning with her head over the toilet bowl?'

Zoey smiled. She loved Hazel's irreverent sense of humour, and the fact that she still had it even though she was suffering was a marvel. And though she had registered that George and his guys had been strapping young men in their early twenties, she'd not really had the time to properly notice. Her head had been filled with other things. Had anything broken during transport? Would she ever find all her important documents ever again? How long was it going to take to unpack her life?

'Morning sickness bad today?'

'You're telling me. I've tried ginger tea, I've tried sniffing a lemon, but I'm getting so acquainted with my bathroom I'm thinking of installing a television. Can I pop round? Help you unpack?'

'Are you in any condition to do so?'

'No, but it usually gets better by mid-afternoon, so I could supervise until then.'

'Well, if you're sure? I could use your advice on something.'

'As long as it's not anti-sickness measures. Give me ten more minutes to squeeze out whatever's left in my stomach and then I'll be right round.'

'You make it sound like a dream.' Zoey chuckled.

'Nightmare more like. See you in a bit.'

She got off the phone and hurried up the stairs to assess the boxes and suitcases in her bedroom. She could barely move in there. How did she have so much stuff? Why hadn't she decluttered before she'd moved?

At least she could get Hazel's advice when she got here. It would be good to see her sister. She'd not really seen her since Brad's funeral. Life had simply got in the way.

*'Would you like to join me for supper?'*

Erin had paused at the end of the pathway, totally unaware that the invitation had been about to come out of her mouth. What had she been thinking? Had her brain imploded or something? She'd been trying to get away and the last time she'd checked, getting away from someone did not involve asking them out for supper! But in the short distance from the front door to the end of the path, her brain had somehow formulated that Zoey probably wouldn't be cooking for herself tonight. That she would most probably be getting a takeaway. And then, Erin's *traitorous* brain had somehow conjured up a sweet image of them both sitting on the seafront eating chips out of a paper bag, the sea breeze playfully teasing Zoey's beautiful white blonde hair, and it had been *so long* since she'd shared time with a girlfriend, or anyone outside of work, and before she knew it she was asking Zoey out for supper.

*Like an idiot!*

And she'd had to stand there, watching the surprise cross Zoey's face, because, let's face it, even *she* probably thought it was weird, and then she'd said, '*That'd be great!*' and now she'd have to find something to do until six o'clock, so that she didn't hyperfocus on what an idiotic thing she had just done.

Hadn't she vowed to never complicate her life again? Hadn't she decided to keep herself to herself from now on? Hadn't she promised herself that after the whole sorry debacle with Jenna she would only go to work or attend work-like events? Where the order of the day was business. *Distance* was her word for the year.

Erin didn't need any more friends. She had plenty of those and they were all nicely coupled up and that was perfect. She did not need to be socializing with a beautiful single woman like Zoey who *lived next door*! And who was probably straight anyway.

There was no doubt a long and tragic list of relationships in Zoey's life. The fact that she'd moved here alone testified to that. Failed marriage? Disappointing boyfriends? Difficult divorce? Could be any or all of them.

Erin made herself go out at lunchtime. She got into her car and drove down into Westcombe. She picked up a sandwich from a shop then went and found a bench up on the headland to sit and eat, looking out over the blue sea that sparkled in the sunshine. This was a good spot to view all of Westcombe. She'd once come up here and painted it, using watercolours. Erin didn't think she was any good at the actual painting part but she adored the peace that would wash over her whilst she tried to create. That was what she did it for. It was like a meditation. Dipping the brush into the glass of water, swiping the brush over a colour, mixing it with another on the palette and then applying it to the paper, watching as the wet paint seeped into the paper, spreading in all directions. Cleaning her brush by dipping it into water and watching the colour leech away again…so peaceful.

It slowed her mind, which had a tendency to race on occasion.

*I mean, look at this morning.*

Here she was, sitting on a bench eating a sandwich because she'd lied about having a lunch date so she'd had to come out, and tonight she'd be sharing a supper with Zoey. Where, in all of her careful planning to keep her distance from people, had that little invitation snuck in from? And was it too late to duck out of the obligation? Say something had come up? Or that she was on call?

*And lie some more?*

Erin hated lying. She hated people lying to her and she hated lying to others. Maybe this supper date was penance for some reason, but hey, all she had to do was get through an hour or two of being polite with her new neighbour and new colleague. That was all. She wasn't surprised any more. She wasn't shocked. Her brain had had time now to calm down and not react out of character and it would stick to the rules from now on.

It was takeaway with a colleague. A fellow professional. A neighbour. She could think of it as a work do. People did that and it was nothing special. She could keep it that way, too.

So what if Zoey was attractive?

So what that she seemed nice?

Jenna had been that way too, and look how that had turned out!

Erin refused to be taken in by a pretty smile and bright blue eyes.

*Not a chance in hell.*

'Mmm…perfect!' Zoey used the small wooden fork to break apart her battered fish. The aroma of freshly fried batter, fish, salt and vinegar dizzied her hungry and tired senses. After a long day of unpacking, sorting and hefting heavy boxes about she was exhausted! And all she truly wanted after this was to go back to Seaglass Cottage, fill up the bath with bubbles and soak in it with a nice glass of wine before bed.

But first, food. She was starving! And these fish and chips looked like they were going to hit the spot for sure.

They'd found a small spot on the beachfront. There was a low wall that ran along the back with benches and though the beach was packed with tourists and holidaymakers they'd managed to squeeze into a space on the far left.

Above them seagulls cried their greed as they swooped around looking for morsels and in front of them children laughed and played, hopping over the gentle waves rippling in to shore or sitting on the sand, building castles, their parents and family either stretched out on brightly coloured towels beside them or reclining in deckchairs with books and tablets, reading. Bikini straps lowered around shoulders on the women, men lying flat out, eyes closed.

'You can't beat fish and chips eaten outdoors,' Erin agreed.

'Thank you for inviting me. I probably would have just sat indoors eating, but this is much better.'

Hazel hadn't stayed long. It had been so nice to see her sister and give her a long hug. It had been way too long since they'd seen one another, even if they had been in touch via the phone. She'd felt so guilty about that. All the times she'd promised to try and make it down to Westcombe to see her sister but something had always cropped up. Work. Brad's parents. They'd been particularly needy since their son's death and she'd always felt obliged to go and see them when they called. Zoey understood. She was their last remaining connection to their son and being around her made them feel that Brad was still there. But their needs had made her neglect her own.

Her need to move on. To breathe. She had

become so stifled, so ensnared by their parental grief that she'd had to break free. They'd not been happy when they'd heard the news that she was going to move away.

*'But what will we do without you here?'*

Zoey knew she'd made the right choice for herself, but had she been selfish? So, sitting at home alone, surrounded by disarray and boxes, eating by herself, probably wouldn't have been the best idea. Not on a day when she was still feeling so guilty. Saturdays had always been spent with Serena and Geoffrey, Brad's parents, and this was the first one in nearly two years that she was not with them. It was why she'd booked the move for the Saturday, so that the day would be filled and she'd have too much to think about so her thoughts didn't linger on them.

Her neighbour Jack had reminded her a little of own father, though, so that had been nice. And Erin? Well, she was clearly a very kind soul, asking her out to supper. She seemed so well put together! Where did the chaos reside in Erin Bramley?

'So, tell me about the practice. Anything I need to know that wouldn't have been shared with me at the interview?' she asked with a smile.

A piece of flaky fish broke away from Erin's fork as she put it in her mouth and she used a finger to lift the flake and suck it from her finger. 'Erm, well, let's see…there's Keiko, the practice manager, who I assume you met during the interviews. She's very good and has got all of our backs. She's not the type to hide away in her office. She deals with problems instantly and she's really keen on making sure there's a supportive atmosphere.'

'Sounds great. Is there a but?'

'No, not really. She just does this thing though, when we all have a practice meeting. She likes everyone to be receptive and zen, so she insists on starting each meeting with us all closing our eyes and having a minute of silence. I thought it was weird when I first started there, but I've got used to it now. It can just be a surprise when you start.' Erin smiled. 'We have a very efficient reception supervisor, Polly. Honestly, the woman never sits down. She's even got one of those standing desk things, so she's on her feet from the second she arrives in the morning until five thirty when she goes home. What about your last practice? What was that like?'

'Quietly busy. Good people mostly, though one of the partners, Dr Latimer, was a bit prickly.'

'How so?'

'I'm not sure, exactly. I was there for years and felt that I never really knew the guy. He rebuffed all attempts to get to know him. If you met him in the staff room making tea or lunch or whatever, he would confine conversation to work or just scurry away and act like he'd never seen you. It was weird. But his patients loved him, so I guess that's all that matters.'

'What made you decide to leave and come to Westcombe?'

How much to say, to share? Should she take a leaf out of Dr Latimer's book and not give details? But she wanted to be honest. Why try to have a fresh start but hide things? She should just be herself.

'I needed a change. Two years ago, I lost my husband, Brad. Sudden cardiac arrest, completely unexpected. And since then I've kind of felt trapped, like I couldn't breathe, and my sister, Hazel, who moved down here years ago, suggested I get a place here to be closer to her.' She forked a chip. 'She's pregnant, no partner, and I wanted us to be close again, so...here I am!'

'Your sister lives in Westcombe?'

'Yep.'

'What's her surname?'

'Wilson.'

'Hazel Wilson.' Erin nodded. 'She's my patient. I remember her coming to me to confirm the pregnancy. I can see the resemblance!'

'Yeah? She's suffering terribly with morning sickness still, poor thing.'

'I'm sorry to hear about your husband. How long were you together?'

'Fifteen years. We met at university.'

'You must have been very young.'

'Twenty years old. Of course, everyone told us we were too young and that getting married whilst at uni was a dumb thing to do, but…' Zoey thought back to those confusing years where she was trying to find out who she was.

She'd felt so confused. Unsure of her sexuality. Her first date was with a girl. Violet. She'd seemed so cool. So different to everyone else with her pink-blonde hair, multiple ear piercings and laconic attitude and yet at the same time so sweet and kind and funny to be with. She'd imagined all through the date what it might be like to kiss her. And whether she was brave enough to. They'd gone to the cinema, sat together in the darkness, and Violet had reached for Zoey's hand. Then Violet had leaned over. Kissed her. Zoey had never felt joy like it! The date had gone so well. They'd gone back to Zoey's halls and there'd been a passionate encounter. Zoey had thought that maybe this was the start of something special. But in the morning Violet wasn't there any more, she'd ghosted her, and Zoey had been so upset.

She could remember crying one day in the quad and then this guy had passed her a real handkerchief and it was Brad and he'd just sat and listened to her. After that he'd become a good friend. A shoulder to lean on. A safe space. He'd scooped her up when she was low, made her feel better about herself again, and her feelings for him had made her even more confused. It wasn't a passionate relationship but he'd made her feel safe, secure, loved, and though physically it had been okay, there were never any fireworks. But after the uncertainty of Violet, that had seemed like a good thing, a sensible thing, and at the time she'd placed more value on knowing where she stood. On knowing upon whom she could rely. And that was Brad. So when he'd offered her his world, his life, his love, his ring on her finger, she'd said yes.

Maybe saying yes had been a dumb thing to do. Brad had been her rebound, but she'd been so terrified to feel confused and alone that it had just seemed easier to get swept up in the excitement of planning a wedding.

'How about you? How did you end up in Westcombe?'

Erin shrugged. 'I didn't intend to. I'd always worked as a locum and I came here to Westcombe originally to cover a six-week period and ended up staying. Got offered a permanent position and thought, why not? I like the area. The people.'

Zoey noticed how Erin's eyes darkened when she mentioned liking the people. What was that about? Had someone upset her someplace else? Whatever it was, it wasn't her place to probe and she wanted to keep their conversation light.

'I used to come here for holidays as a child. I think that's why Hazel moved out here. Because of the happy memories.'

'My family came here once, too. They had a campervan that they could extend with a tent. Horrible thing it was. We were never warm at night.' Erin smiled as she remembered. 'I loved donkey rides the best.'

Zoey smiled too. 'So did I.'

There was a squeal from down on the beach, then the sound of a young child crying. They watched as a young mother and father got to their feet and scooped up their child, who seemed to be about eighteen months old, and then began to look as if they were panicking and didn't know what to do.

Zoey looked at Erin and they put down their fish and chips and ran over to the family.

'What happened?'

The mother was panicking, holding her crying baby to her chest. 'He crawled over the barbecue! He's burned his hands!'

'We're doctors. Let us take a look,' Erin said, her voice calm and assured, her tone instructive. Taking charge. Something that was needed amongst the panic the parents were feeling.

The toddler did not want anyone looking at his hands but it was clear that there was a burn on both palms.

'Have you got water?' Zoey asked.

'What? Yes! In the cooler!' the dad answered, turning to the icebox they had and ripping off the lid. He grabbed a bottle of water from one of many.

Erin took the lid off the bottle and poured the water over the toddler's hands. 'With the other bottles, empty them out into the cooler. All of them. We're going to sit this little one in there. When you've done that, call for an ambulance.'

The toddler's skin was beginning to blister. Zoey could see it, red and raw, the poor thing, and though the little boy did not want his mother to put him down, Zoey helped her place her son in the cooler so he could sit in the water and keep his hands beneath the surface, even though he kept trying to pull them up and cry.

'Does he have any health conditions we need to know about?' Zoey asked the panicking, crying mother.

She shook her head.

'You're visiting? On holiday?' It was a distraction technique. She knew that all the mother wanted to do was scoop her son up and hold him, but she had to get her focused on other things.

'Yes.'

'Okay. I know you want to hold him, but Dr Bramley needs to hold his hands down in the water like that to help cool the skin, okay?'

The father stood a way off on the phone, one finger plugged into his ear to cut out the noise from the beach and crowd that had gathered to watch. 'Yes. On a barbecue,' she heard him say to the ambulance dispatcher. 'Yes. Please hurry!'

'Has he got a favourite toy?' Zoey asked the mum.

'Yeah. A duck.'

'Do you want to get that for him to hold? Maybe gather your things for when the ambulance gets here. Don't worry. We've got him, okay?'

The dad nodded and began to frantically assemble their belongings as the mum kept whispering soothing things to her still distraught son, kissing his sweaty head of hair.

By Zoey's reckoning, this was a second degree partial thickness burn she could see. And though it was horrible for the parents and the child, it was a good thing that he could feel the pain, because it meant the boy hadn't burned through his nerve-endings. He would likely recover quite well from this; it was just traumatic in the here and now.

They kept the parents busy and talking and Zoey took it in turns with Erin to hold the boy's hands underneath the cool water until the ambulance arrived, screaming onto the seafront alongside the seagulls whirling overhead. Of course it caused a scene. Everyone was watching. But Zoey was so impressed with how Erin was, talking to the poor toddler and being so reassuring.

Erin and Zoey relayed what medical knowledge they had of the boy to the paramedics when they arrived, who were able to wrap the burns in cling film as they got the boy and his mother into the ambulance, the dad promising to follow in his car.

When it was all over and the ambulance had disappeared from sight, Erin turned to Zoey and sighed. 'Welcome to Westcombe!'

# CHAPTER THREE

WESTCOMBE BAY MEDICAL PRACTICE was situated on Harbour Lane, about fifty metres back from the seafront. Above, the ever-present seagulls whirled in the air, crying out to one another as Zoey got out from her car and locked it. Behind the practice, there seemed to be a small nature trail and already she could see people walking along it with their dogs.

She was looking forward to her first day, but was also nervous. She'd not had a first day at work for such a long time, she'd forgotten how it could feel. The nerves in her belly, the anticipation, the need to just get stuck in and start helping people.

She'd already done that, of course, at the weekend, helping that poor toddler with the accidental hand burns after he'd crawled onto a discarded disposable barbecue that was still hot. But she'd called the hospital the next day to get an update and though they couldn't tell her personal details, the doctor was able to tell her that the boy was going to be just fine. And that was all she needed to know. She would pass the news on to Erin when she saw her.

The idea of seeing her again made her heart beat a little faster. She liked Erin very much. After the incident on the beach they'd returned home and when they'd got out of Erin's car there'd been a moment. Awkward as hell, but still friendly.

*'Thanks for supper.'*

Erin had nodded and laughed, her face lighting with amusement. *'No problem. Though I think it must be said that not all my supper invitations are usually that dramatic.'*

Zoey had laughed too, marvelling at the way the evening sun bounced light across Erin's face. Hoping that she wasn't staring too hard. Hoping that Erin didn't notice how Zoey was fascinated by the light across Erin's mouth, casting her lower, fuller lip into slight shadow, making it look…well…*kissable.*

The thought was alarming. Accelerated her pulse and made her feel all hot and uncomfortable. She knew she needed to say goodbye, so she could hurry into her cottage and think about Erin's lips.

*No! I didn't mean that!*

*I meant...oh, dammit.*

Zoey was a hugger. It was how she said hello,

how she said goodbye, and so she'd lunged in to give Erin a quick hug, intending it to last only a second, nothing more, but the second she'd felt Erin in her arms, inhaled her scent, felt her soft body against her own, she'd felt the heat rise up in her neck and into her face and, embarrassed, she'd let go and stepped away and rummaged for her keys and told Erin she'd see her on Monday.

But all through Sunday she'd found herself keeping an eye on her neighbour's back garden to see if Erin went into it. She hadn't, of course, and Zoey had tried to keep herself occupied unpacking some more boxes, trying to sort out her life, what she wanted to keep, what she could get rid of, and she'd got stuck on a box of framed photos. Her and Brad on their wedding day. Brad's parents, Serena and Geoffrey. At her old home they'd been in pride of place on the mantelpiece, but she didn't want to do that here. They needed to go someplace else, but where? And because she couldn't make up her mind, she'd called Hazel for a chat and after that she went to look out into the back garden again, hoping to be distracted by Erin.

'Morning, Zoey.'

She turned at Erin's voice, as if thinking about her had somehow magically conjured her up out of thin air. But no, Erin was just getting out of her own car, which must have pulled up and parked whilst Zoey had been daydreaming about the weekend.

'Morning! Sorry, I was miles away.'

'Thinking happy thoughts?'

'Kind of.' She couldn't tell Erin that she'd been thinking about *her*.

'Ready for your first day?'

Zoey nodded. 'As I'll ever be. I just want it to go smoothly, you know?' She couldn't help but notice how wonderful Erin looked today. A charcoal grey pencil skirt, a crushed pink silk blouse. Legs to die for, ending in the most amazing pair of heels that Zoey had ever seen. Her outfit made Zoey feel dowdy in comparison. A simple white blouse, black trousers. Flat ballet pumps, because she'd wanted to be comfortable.

'Well, any questions, don't hesitate to ask. Are you seeing Keiko first thing?'

'I think so. I'm going to get a quick orientation and then make a start on my list.'

'Well, I'll show you the most important thing,' Erin said, laying a hand lightly on Zoey's forearm.

'What's that?' She tried to ignore the tingling she felt at Erin's touch.

'Where the kettle is!'

They both laughed and began to walk in together, the doors sliding open at their approach.

There was very much a nautical theme outside the practice, with a small shingle area with a small old rowing boat out front, filled with flowers. An old anchor leaned against the wall beneath a window and opposite the main doors was an old wooden memorial bench, fitted with a metal plaque with a dedication.

'That was for Dr Morely. He passed a few years ago, apparently.'

'You never met him?'

'Here before my time, sadly. But every patient sings his praises. I'd like to think that when it's my time, my patients will feel the same way about me.'

'Well, let's hope it's not your time yet!' Zoey said, eyebrow raised jokingly.

'Good point.'

Inside, there was a reception manned by three receptionists, one at the main desk and two off to the side, taking the phone calls that were already coming in and dealing with admin and prescription requests.

Erin gave them a quick wave and Zoey smiled a polite hello. 'I'll show you where the kettle is, and once we've got you armed with a cup of tea we'll take you to Keiko's office.'

'Perfect.'

The staff room was small. A tiny kitchenette area, a sofa, low coffee table and two single chairs. Erin introduced Zoey to the advanced nurse practitioner, Darren, who seemed lovely, and then Erin grabbed two mugs. 'Tea or coffee?'

'Tea, please.'

'Milk and sugar?'

'Just milk, thanks.'

'Sweet enough, huh?' Erin clicked on the kettle.

Zoey smiled. *Maybe!*

When the drinks were made, Erin passed over her mug and when she went to take it, their fingers brushed. Just for a moment, but long enough for Zoey to notice. She had to admit to being slightly in awe of Erin. She was accomplished, clever, kind, stylish, and incredibly beautiful. The fact that she appeared to be single was staggering. Was it a choice on her part? Or was there something in her past keeping her single and alone? Not that she seemed lonely. Clearly, she had a social life, she'd gone out to lunch with someone at the weekend, so maybe Zoey was wrong. Maybe Erin was dating and keeping that to herself. She had every right, and why would she have shared that with Zoey when they'd only just met? She'd not shared everything about Brad.

At the thought of Brad, her phone in her pocket buzzed and she pulled it out and glanced at the screen. A text message from his parents.

Let us know how the first day goes. Serena x

Zoey pushed the phone back into her pocket. No *Best wishes on your first day*? No *Good luck*? No. *Let them know how it went*, the sub-text being, *If it goes badly, you can always come back.* Serena and Geoffrey had *not* been happy at her selling up and trying to break away.

'Let's get you to Keiko,' Erin said.

Keiko Kobiyashi had a nice office next to the staff room, dominated by a large desk in the centre, filled with all the accoutrements a person would expect from a practice manager. Desktop computer and monitor, desk diary splayed open right in front of her, inbox and outbox, an outgoing mail tray, and around her, a room filled with filing cabinets, on top of which sat a row of box files, all neatly ordered by year. Certificates lined the wall and behind her, on the windowsill, were some pictures of Keiko and her family, most notably two little boys who looked to be about five and seven.

'Dr Marsh! Good morning. I had no idea you'd arrived already.' Keiko got to her feet and came around the desk to shake Zoey's hand. 'I see you've met Dr Bramley?'

Zoey nodded. 'We met on Saturday. She's my next-door neighbour.'

'Really? I guess you two can start car-pooling then?' She laughed and stepped back behind her desk. 'Take a seat.'

'I'll leave you both to it. Any problems, Zoey, don't hesitate to knock on my door.'

Zoey nodded and smiled her thanks, feeling the air go out of her lungs a little at Erin's departure. Something about having her by her side made her feel stronger. More confident. Was it because of what had happened on the beach on Saturday evening? Working with her to care for that young boy had made them quickly depend upon one another. It had trauma bonded them.

'It's lovely to have you here at last, Zoey. It is all right to call you Zoey?'

'Of course!'

'Having you here brings us back up to having a full team of doctors and medical staff and I don't need to tell you how important that can be for a practice.'

No, she didn't. Not enough doctors or nurses meant that patients had to wait longer for treatment, and nobody wanted that. It was always better to prevent something than to have to try and cure it.

'As you're so experienced, I'm not going to have you shadow anyone on your first day. You've used our computer system before at your old practice, so you are familiar with the IT, but I have given you fifteen minutes per patient instead of the normal ten for this first week, just until you get to know where everything is and get familiar with our procedures.'

'All right.'

'There is a welcome folder in your consulting room, which is fully equipped and ready. It includes your parking permit, so you might want to go and put that in your car before you start.'

'Okay.'

'The rest of it is policies, procedures, the ethos of the practice, safeguarding, that kind of thing. There's information about the shared drives, passwords, log-in IDs, governance…' Keiko frowned as if to see if she could remember anything else. 'But if you have any questions, I'll be in all day. Do you have any questions for me right now?'

'I can't think of any.'

'Good. So shall we show you your room and give you a tour?'

'That'd be great. Thanks.'

'Glad to have you on board!'

Erin closed the door to her consultation room and then leaned back against it with a sigh. She was trying her very best to be friendly and kind and supportive to Zoey, but every moment she spent with her left her feeling like she wanted more, like she wanted to linger and just stare at her face, or watch the way she moved, and she didn't need this extra complication! Whatever it was.

Why was she feeling this way? She barely knew the woman, but after Saturday's adventure on the beach with that poor little boy, Erin had hidden in her home all day on Sunday, afraid that if she went out she'd somehow run into Zoey again and have to force herself to not keep staring at her.

Zoey had no idea how beautiful she was. It was clear in the way she moved, the way she acted. Even bare of make-up, she was naturally stunning and that white blonde hair of hers, the way it fell in soft, gentle waves, brushing her shoulders… Erin had forced away the images in her head of stepping up behind Zoey, gently pulling that hair to one side to brush her lips over Zoey's soft skin…

'Stop it. Stop it now,' she said out loud, ordering herself to be rational, to get her head into gear and ready for work. Zoey had been married to a man! For years! And if she was attracted to guys as well as girls, then that made her even more like her ex. And all she had to do was remind herself of what Jenna had done to her and she wasn't going to go through that again. And most certainly not with a woman who was not only her brand-new colleague at the practice but also her next-door neighbour!

She slung her bag over the hook on the back of the door, slumped into her seat and switched on the computer, tapping in her passwords to access the systems she needed. She had to get her head back in the game. Ignore the fact that Zoey would be right next door in Dr Mullin's old room. A vast improvement on the locum that had been filling in for weeks just recently, and she'd only known Zoey for two days.

The first patient on her list was a young woman who was coming in for her six-week mother and baby check. Erin sucked in a breath and let it out. Babies were always difficult for her to deal with. She called them through and the mother arrived, looking suitably tired yet presentable, whilst pushing a pram that contained her baby. 'Morning, Jackie. How are you doing?'

Jackie closed the consulting room door behind her, then settled herself in the seat beside Erin's desk. 'I'm good! Really good.'

'Glad to hear it. And baby?'

'He's doing well, too. Well, I hope he is! He's my first, so we're both navigating these new waters together.'

Erin scanned Jackie's birth notes. She'd had a vaginal delivery at thirty-nine weeks and six days. Epidural. Second degree tear. Normal blood loss. She'd received a rhesus injection because her baby's blood was O positive and Jackie was A negative. Baby was born weighing eight pounds and seven ounces with a good APGAR score and was being breastfed. APGAR was a mnemonic used by maternity units to assess a baby's condition after birth. It created a score-based system, the highest mark being ten, that assessed appearance, pulse, grimace, activity and respiration to determine if a baby needed help after delivery.

'Okay, well, shall we assess you first, seeing as he's sleeping right now? How are you feeling in general?'

'I'm tired. But that's the nights, I'm guessing.'

'He's waking you to feed often, or just crying?'

'I think he cries until he gets me. He doesn't really want to feed, it seems, he just likes the security of suckling at the nipple. Mind you, he made me really sore to start with. They got all cracked and it was painful.'

'It can be. Especially the first time you breastfeed. How are you doing with that now?'

'Better. I got nipple guards and used a cream that the health visitor recommended.'

'Good. And down below? Still bleeding or has that stopped?'

'There's a tiny bit, but not much. I'm still wearing a pad, but it's not really blood. More like a peachy colour.'

'That sounds like the tail-end of it. What about your mood? How would you rate that?'

'It's all right. I can be weepy sometimes at television adverts that pull on the heartstrings, but I think I'm okay.'

'Well, I'm going to get you to fill in a questionnaire, just so we can measure that, if that's okay?'

Erin ran through the questionnaire with Jackie and was relieved to see that she didn't seem to be suffering from postnatal depression. 'Okay. Are you all right to pop up onto the bed so I can check you and then we'll look at Arlo?'

'Of course.'

There was no sign of mastitis in Jackie and she was right; her nipples had adapted to the feeding of her son. Vaginally, her stitches were healing nicely and Jackie confirmed that she wasn't having any trouble with going to the toilet. All was well with mum. Now it was time for Arlo. 'Do you want to get him out and undress him for me?'

She watched as Jackie scooped her son up from beneath his blankets and smiled at the way little Arlo's scrunched-up body seemed to resist being disturbed from his sleep. How his face went red and his mouth opened in protest. But all it took was a few soothing words from his mum and a quick cuddle and he settled down and seemed to accept the fact that he was now being undressed down to his nappy.

Erin stepped forward to begin her examination. Arlo was very handsome. Cute, with clear eyes and good skin tone. She talked to him in a sing-song way as she examined him—there were no rashes, pimples or abnormalities. She checked his hip flexion, umbilical area, his spine and bottom. His testes were checked, his hands, his feet. A thorough checkup to ensure nothing was missed at birth. ‘You’re perfect, aren’t you? Yes, you are,’ she said, lifting him off the examination bed and holding him in her arms for a moment.

To think she’d been so close once to having a baby with Jenna, only for it to be so cruelly snatched away at the end from betrayal. She’d missed out on all of this. It had been stolen from her, but life was unfair and she’d been through enough therapy by now to know that she had to let that go. To let Jenna live her life. To accept that she was alone now and would forever be. These moments, with patients’ babies, would be the closest she would ever have to holding her own child.

‘We’ll need to get Arlo booked in for his eight-week vaccinations. Are you happy for me to book those onto the system?’

Jackie smiled and nodded.

'Any questions about those that worry you at all?'

'No. Not at all.'

'We'll talk you through them when you bring Arlo in, but basically, it'll be the six-in-one vaccine. It's given at eight, twelve and sixteen weeks of age. The six-in-one covers baby for diphtheria, hepatitis B, hib, polio, tetanus and whooping cough. And he'll also receive vaccinations for rotavirus, which protects against diarrhoea and vomiting. He'll get the second vaccination for that at twelve weeks. Then there's the Men B vaccine, which requires follow-up shots at twelve weeks and one year. I've got a leaflet I can give you explaining them all in more detail and why they're important. I know it can sound overwhelming at the moment.'

'Thank you.'

'I guess, Arlo, I need to give you back to Mummy, so she can dress you.' It had been nice to hold a baby in her arms again and she always felt a little sad handing them back. Their little Babygros were so cute! So small!

She got out the information and placed it on her desk and began typing up her notes as Jackie dressed her son. It always felt good when these examinations went well. She hated when she noticed a problem, knowing what a worry it would be for the parents and family. But that hadn't been a worry for today, thankfully.

'Have you thought about contraception, moving forward?'

'We're going to use condoms.'

'That's good. But if you ever want a different method, you can always book into one of our wellness clinics and, as usual, if you have any concerns, do give us a call.'

'Thank you, Doctor.'

'Take care. Bye.' She waved them off with a smile and returned to her patient record, recording her observations of both mum and baby. But she couldn't help but think back to holding little Arlo. Such a tiny person. So full of future and possibility. Who would he grow up to be? What would her life have been like if Jenna had not gone behind her back? If they'd persevered a little while longer? Maybe they'd have a baby right now and Erin would be a mother. She would not be going home to an empty cottage but one filled with family, with love, with adoration and the beautiful windy smiles of a baby. That baby smell. Bottles and bathtimes and simply standing by a cot and gazing down at a child and marvelling at how much they loved one another.

But it had not gone that way. Jenna had cheated. Breaking them apart. Stealing the future from her. Her home was empty and she was alone and lonely. Her next patient had not yet arrived and so she decided to distract herself with fulfilling prescription requests and reading a letter from a consultant about one of her patients.

She refused to wallow in the misery and mess that Jenna had created.

At lunchtime, Zoey decided that she would take a walk down to the seafront and eat her sandwiches there, in the sunshine and fresh air. Back in Guildford, she'd often eaten at her desk and ploughed through admin at the same time, or, more often than not, attended home visits for housebound patients, squeezing in a quick lunch when she got back. But here? She was determined to make sure she took a proper lunch for herself and a break from her screen.

'Headed on out?' Erin called out as Zoey passed her door.

'Thought I'd eat my sandwiches by the harbour. Fancy coming along?'

Erin reluctantly shook her head. 'I'd love to, but I've had a home visit request last minute. You could come with me. Eat your food in the car.'

And even though she'd been looking forward to getting some fresh air and relaxing by looking out at the water, the invitation wasn't one she wanted to turn down. She could spend some time with her new friend Erin, decompress and still get lunch, so why not?

'Great!'

'Perfect. I'll just grab the patient summary from Reception and we can go.'

Outside, the sun was shining and it was yet another beautiful summer's day. The skies were blue and cloudless, a warm, gentle breeze occasionally blew, lifting Erin's honey blonde hair as she walked by Zoey's side, but when her hair fell, it seemed to naturally return to a perfect state, a long, groomed wave. Zoey didn't have hair like that.

'What's your secret?' she asked.

Erin looked at her quizzically. 'Secret?'

'To perfect hair. We've been outside less than a minute and mine's already flyaway and all over the place,' she said, tucking stray strands that kept catching across her cheeks and lips to behind her ears.

Erin laughed self-consciously, patting her hair down. 'Oh, it's not perfect, believe me. It takes me hours to tame it,' she said, sounding self-deprecating. 'Besides, your hair is gorgeous! What are you going on about?'

Zoey blushed, knowing that Erin was only trying to make her feel better, but the truth was that only one of them got into Erin's car not looking like they'd been pulled through a gorse-bush backwards and it wasn't Zoey. But still, it was nice to hear a compliment about it. She'd always been so self-conscious about her hair. It had always been white blonde and it had always been quite messy. As a child, her mum would have to plait Zoey's hair every day before school, but she'd still get teased for it. Other kids pulling her hair, saying she was weird. It had made her self-conscious. As she'd grown older, she'd tried dyeing it different colours, but they'd never seemed to take that well, so then she'd taken to wearing a lot of hats. Berets. Scarves. Brad had called it her movie starlet era. He had always joked about how paranoid she was about her hair. So, for Erin to say it was gorgeous? Zoey hoped that she meant it.

'Thank you. That's very kind,' she said, running her fingers through the tangles, trying to sort it out but failing.

Erin noticed her struggling to tame the back. 'Here. Let me.'

And suddenly Erin was leaning over, her hands and fingers in Zoey's hair, gently teasing the tangles out.

Zoey sucked in a breath and went very still at Erin's touch. Her cheeks flamed like a furnace, her mouth dry as her heart thudded so hard she thought it could be heard in the small confines of the car.

'There you go.' Erin smiled, smoothing down Zoey's hair, meeting her gaze. A moment of awareness. A moment in which Erin seemed to realise how close she'd been and what an intimate thing that could have been interpreted as, and she blushed and settled back in her own seat, starting the engine of her car.

'Thanks.' Zoey subconsciously smoothed her hair, too, running her fingers over the spot where Erin's hands had been moments ago. But she couldn't linger on what that moment had felt like. What it had inspired. How her body had reacted to Erin's touch. 'Who are we going to see?' she asked, keen to return the moment to something professional and distancing herself from how her body had come alive.

'Mrs Pearl Wallace. She's eighty-seven years old and she's terminally ill with a lung cancer that's spread to her neck, liver and bones.'

'Poor thing.'

'She had her own place, but her daughter, Sylvia, moved her into her own home to look after her when she got sick.'

'What's the reason for the callout today?'

'Sylvia wants her mum's pain levels assessed again as she's worried that the morphine isn't doing as well. She is on a lower dose at the moment, so there is room still to increase it. She just wants to make sure she doesn't give her too much.'

Zoey nodded. She understood. Time was precious when you were looking after someone who was terminal. You wanted them to be comfortable and pain-free and to sleep when they needed. But you also hoped for moments in which you could spend time with them and have them present enough to understand and talk with you, if they could.

'Have you known them long?'

Erin nodded. 'Since Pearl got diagnosed. But when she did it was already stage four and had metastasized. She did have surgery that left her with a stoma bag, but we've lost systemic control of the cancer and so now we're just trying to keep her comfortable. It's a bit unsettling. I lost a patient at the weekend to the same thing.'

'I'm sorry to hear that. How's Sylvia coping?'

'She's doing well. She's stoic. Making the best of the situation as much as she can. I've tried to put her in touch with support groups and people to talk to, but she says that's not her thing and besides, she doesn't like the idea of leaving her mum with carers so she can attend these things. The Macmillan Nurses are great with her, though, and they visit the house to provide her with emotional and mental support.'

'That's good.'

Erin glanced at her. 'Why don't you eat your lunch? It's a good ten-minute drive.'

'When will you eat?'

'When I get back to the practice.'

'I'll eat mine with you, then.' It seemed the polite thing to do.

Erin's smile warmed Zoey's heart. She could tell that in Erin she was going to have a great friend and that these weird feelings she kept having about her were just fleeting and her admiration and infatuation at having met someone who seemed so wonderful and well put-together was just that. Fleeting. It would go. These feelings were only because for the first time in a long time she felt as if *she* was being seen. Her. Zoey. Not Brad's wife. Not as a daughter-in-law who was needed to salve a parents' loss. Not as a doctor who could help someone. Erin *saw* Zoey.

And it was nice.

More than nice. It felt novel. Exciting. *Liberating.*

Happy, she took the time to look out of the window and admire the views of Westcombe as Erin drove.

The old fishing village was pretty much exactly as she remembered it from childhood. It really hadn't changed much and seemed caught in a bit of a time warp. But that was lovely. It felt like a traditional seaside place. Fish and chip shops on the seafront. Old arcades for youngsters. The curve of the harbour wall cradling the fishing boats. The bright arc of beach, nestled between two headlands. There was a Monday market on today and so Erin took a different road to avoid it, but not before Zoey caught a glimpse of a stall selling art prints and box frames filled with seaglass to form people or lighthouses or beach huts. She made a note that next Monday, if she wasn't doing any house visits herself, she would come out to the market at lunchtime and have a wander around. Maybe find a few bits for the cottage? Decorate with new things, rather than items that used to be hers and Brad's.

'Here we are.'

The car pulled to a stop on a small road, lined with smart bungalows, laburnum and silver-birch trees. They got out together and, side by side, walked up the garden path and Erin rang the doorbell, glancing at Zoey with a smile.

The door was opened by a woman who appeared to be in her late fifties.

'Hello, Sylvia,' Erin said. 'I've brought Dr Marsh with me. She's new at the practice, just thought it might be good for you and your mum to meet her.'

Sylvia, dark hair cut into a neat bob, gave Zoey a nod. 'Hello. Thank you so much for coming, Erin. Mum's been struggling today.' Sylvia stepped back so they could enter.

'Is she in bed?'

'Afraid so. The last few days, actually.'

The bungalow was neat. Tidy. *Minimalist*, Zoey thought. One piece of modern art on the hallway wall and only one photograph on the hallway table. Photos of Sylvia and an older woman, whom Zoey assumed was the mother.

Pearl's bedroom though, was different, filled with memorabilia and photographs. And lying in a proper hospital bed and propped up on a lot of pillows was the patient. Pearl's skin was loose over the prominent bones of her face and her skeletal, liver-spotted hands rested neatly on top of a patchwork quilt in greens and blues.

'Dr Bramley's here, Mum. And Dr Marsh has come to see you, too.'

Pearl turned towards them and tried to manage a smile. 'Oh dear, two doctors…does that mean I'm worse?'

Erin placed her bag on a chair to one side and picked up Pearl's medication file. 'No, no. Dr Marsh is just new, Pearl. She's come to help me decide on how much extra painkiller you might need. Sylvia says it's been getting worse for you and you're not sleeping as well through the night?'

'Oh, you know Sylvia, always making mountains out of molehills.'

'Mum, you're in pain. There's no shame in telling the doctor you need more help.'

Zoey watched Erin carefully. Clearly, they all knew each other quite well, but Erin was managing to maintain her professional distance, despite the traumatic situation and her loss of another patient from the weekend. Zoey knew what it felt like to stand back and feel hopeless whilst someone faded right in front of your eyes. In her case, it had been quick and shocking. Sylvia, on the other hand, was watching her mother die slowly.

Which was worse?

*Maybe they're both just as awful.*

'Pearl? Tell me where it hurts.'

The older woman sighed and began to give them more information, but she still tried her best to play it down. Was the mother saying this to protect her daughter? People made lots of sacrifices for family.

Zoey stepped forward impulsively, even though this was Erin's patient, and sat down on the edge of Pearl's bed, taking the older woman's frail hand in her own. 'Mrs Wallace, I know you want to protect Sylvia from thinking that you're uncomfortable. I get that, I do. But by doing so, it's also causing her pain because she's worrying about you all the time and feeling helpless.

If you can tell us the truth about your pain levels, we can give you enough medication to make you comfortable and also to make Sylvia happy too, knowing that you're not suffering in silence.'

Pearl looked at Erin and smiled. 'She's good, isn't she?'

'She most certainly is.' And Erin meant it.

'Well, Pearl? Out of ten?'

Once Pearl was honest with them and Zoey had adjusted the patient's pillows, she'd comforted Sylvia, whose eyes had welled with tears when she heard the true levels of her mum's pain, Erin was able to prescribe a much higher dose. 'It may make you sleepier, but when you're awake it will make life much more manageable and you should be able to eat and drink more, too,' she said.

'Thank you. I shall try. You know I never imagined I'd end my days like this. I thought my George would still be here with me, but he was taken way before his time. It's odd who ends up holding your hand at the end.'

Outside, after saying goodbye, Zoey looked to Erin. 'What happened to George?'

Erin unlocked the car and they both slid into their seats. 'He was in the army. Had an accident overseas, by all accounts. Apparently, Sylvia was just a baby. Pearl had been waiting for him to come home to meet his daughter for the first time, but he never got the chance.'

'Wow. You never know when your time is up, I guess,' Zoey said.

'No.' Erin paused. 'You were good with her. The way you got Pearl to open up like that.'

'Oh, it was nothing. I just had this realisation that her daughter's happiness was the most important thing to her, so I attacked it from that angle. You'd have done the same if I hadn't got there first.'

'I'm not sure I would have.'

Zoey didn't press the point. Clearly, they had differing approaches. Zoey had sat on Pearl's bed, held her hand, adjusted her blanket for her and her pillows, whereas Erin had stood back, maintained a distance and focused on numbers and drug doses and calculations, hiding behind the numbers.

'You gave her what she needed.'

'Thanks.'

Zoey's stomach rumbled loudly, breaking the sombre tension, and Erin turned up the music in the car as they drove back to the practice. A song came on by a band called Ever True that they both knew and their voices rose together in harmony as they sang along with the lyrics, both of them searching for the joy and the happiness as a defence, a barrier against the dark mood of approaching death that they'd been in moments before.

Back at the practice, they both sat outside on the grass to eat their lunch quickly. Near to them was a large buddleia bush, glorious in its purple blooms and honeyed scent, that attracted a mass of butterflies in all their bright colours and loud, noisy bumblebees searching for nectar.

'Every time I come out here I tell myself I should paint that,' Erin said.

'You paint?' Zoey was surprised.

'I dabble. Watercolours mostly. I'm not good at it, but I enjoy it. I find it soothing sometimes after a difficult day.' Her eyes seemed to darken then.

'I paint too.'

'I thought I saw an easel at your place. What medium do you use?'

'Same as you. Again—' she laughed '—I'm not very good. In fact, sometimes, the results are downright embarrassing and I throw them away instantly, but when I'm doing them it feels good.'

'I'd like to see your art then, some time.'

Zoey blushed. She'd never shown anyone her paintings. Even Brad had never been that interested in seeing the results when she would sometimes take herself off to a beauty spot to dabble with her art. So the fact that Erin wanted to see what she had completed? Well…that was surprising and welcome and…nice.

She fought down the cringe-worthy urge to say *If you show me yours, I'll show you mine* and instead said, 'We should have an art exhibition one day in the waiting room. If we sold anything the money could go to a local charity.'

'Good idea. Though I don't think anyone would part with their hard-earned money to buy my stuff.'

'Hey, art is subjective. You never know who will like what.'

Erin smiled at her. 'You're very good at making other people feel better about themselves, do you know that?'

'Practice makes perfect.'

'And what makes *you* happy?'

The question completely stumped her. Zoey felt like she ought to say something quite deep. Like helping others made her happy and it did, but…she was also here to discover who she was without Brad in her life. Who she used to be. What did make her happy? She wasn't sure she had a real answer. She'd lost who she was over her married years.

In the end, she gave a shrug. 'I guess silly little things that happen in the moment. Serendipity.' She thought a moment longer and decided upon brevity. 'Chocolate!'

Erin laughed. 'Perfect then, because I just so happen to have in my lunchbox two chocolate truffles, hand-crafted by the Westcombe chocolatier. Here.' And she held out her hand. On her outstretched palm sat two gold-wrapped chocolates.

'Thank you!' Zoey went to take one. Her fingertips brushed Erin's skin and she felt a bolt of awareness and electricity rocket up her arm as if she'd touched an outlet. The tingling caused her breath to hitch in her throat and she laughed nervously as she unwrapped it and took a bite.

The chocolate was perfect. Rich, soft and creamy, the hint of hazelnut praline lingering on her tongue. 'Oh my God!'

'Good, aren't they? Cost a fortune, but they really do hit the spot.' Erin closed her eyes in ecstasy, tilting her head back to face the sun as the flavours hit, exposing the soft, creamy length of her throat, and Zoey was suddenly struck by wondering what it would feel like to trace that throat with her tongue.

'Goodness! We'd better get back inside,' she said, standing quickly, gathering her things to banish the naughty and terrifying thought to the back of her mind and then, without thinking, just acting instinctively, she held out her hand to help Erin up.

Erin paused then took it and Zoey pulled her to a standing position.

They were close. Very close. And suddenly aware that they were alone and anything could happen. Erin had a small freckle right near her lips. She tried hard not to stare at Erin's lips but… Embarrassed, she laughed and stepped back—*away, safe*—and fumbled for her belongings, muttering random rubbish.

*'You got everything?'*

*'Lovely day to sit outside.'*

*'Oh, yes, wonderful.'*

It was a relief to be back inside the practice. Zoey busied herself making a mug of tea to take with her into the consulting room for her afternoon list. She didn't notice where Erin went. Off to the bathroom? She took a moment to escape, closing her door behind her and wondering just what the hell she was doing having these thoughts about Erin.

It was one thing to explore who she might be, but she most certainly could not get involved with a colleague! After fifteen years married to a man? That kind of thing…it was too late now, anyway, wasn't it?

*I'm only in my late thirties. Still young, really.*

So why did it feel as if she'd already had her lifetime? Why did it feel as if she'd already had her serious romance in life and anything that came after was just…what? A silly flirtation? And with *a woman*. Zoey had never told her family that she was bisexual. She'd not needed to. The relationship with Violet was over in one day and after that she'd told herself it was just experimenting and then Brad was there and they were getting married and she'd just assumed she would be with him for the rest of her life. There'd been no point in telling people and she'd not even known if her parents would be accepting of that lifestyle, so she'd kept schtum.

Only now she wasn't married any more. Brad had died. And she'd moved here to Westcombe for a fresh start, not to muddy the waters where she lived and worked.

# CHAPTER FOUR

'HAVE YOU HAD your appointments come through for your scans?' Erin was in a consultation with Zoey's sister, Hazel, who'd come in to have her blood pressure checked. She'd been feeling dizzy she said, probably from not being able to keep much food or drink down and the fact that she felt a little dehydrated. But thankfully, her BP had been fine and instead, Erin had discovered that Hazel actually had an ear infection. She'd prescribed amoxicillin.

It had been a week since Zoey had started at the surgery and she had fitted in brilliantly with the team. Everyone liked her very much.

Including Erin. There'd even been one or two moments that had seemed charged between them, but she'd been trying her hardest to brush that off, figuring that she was reading too much into it because she was single and because Zoey was extremely beautiful. It was just biology reacting, that was all. It was natural. Normal to react in that way if someone you were physically attracted to was suddenly in your personal space. But nothing would come of it. There was no way she'd try to see if it could become something more, as she wasn't looking for anything like that. The sting of betrayal still lingered and if something went wrong then that would not only ruin the happiness she'd found here at work, but also in the home she'd created right next door.

Hazel nodded, smiling broadly, eyes twinkling with excitement and anticipation. 'Yes. I've got a scan on Thursday afternoon. Four thirty. My sister is going to go with me.'

Erin smiled. Of course. Hazel didn't have a partner and her and Zoey's parents had emigrated to another country, so of course her sister would go with her. It would be nice for them to do that. To share in the excitement of a new baby in the family. 'That's good.'

She didn't want to feel envious of anyone else's happiness, but it was difficult when everyone else seemed to be starting families or planning them and she was right back at the starting block. Mid-thirties. If she even did ever get brave enough to start dating again, she might not meet someone special for at least a few years and then they'd need time together before they even considered starting a family and by the time they did? They'd be in their mid-forties, probably older than that, and then it all might be too late for Erin to have a family of her own. She'd given her best years to Jenna and then had them count for nothing.

Wasted.

All her prime opportunities gone.

A knock at her door interrupted her regret and she pasted on a smile. 'Come in!'

Zoey opened the door, looking from Erin to Hazel. 'Hey you. Thought I'd pop in and make sure you were okay.' Zoey hugged her sister and then let go, looking her up and down. 'How was your BP?'

'Fine. It's an ear infection. Probably caught it from one of the kids at school. Those places are petri dishes, aren't they?'

'I've prescribed antibiotics,' said Erin.

'Good. Good. And you're all set for Thursday?'

Hazel nodded. 'Yes. Look, I'd better go if I'm going to catch the pharmacy before they close for the day.'

Zoey leant in and kissed her sister on the cheek. 'I'll call you, later.'

'Okay. Bye. Thank you, Dr Bramley.'

'You're welcome.' Erin watched her patient leave, then her gaze returned to her colleague. 'It must be so nice to be close with your sister.'

Zoey nodded. 'It is. I'd not seen her for such

a long time. You know how it is when you get busy and you each get your own lives.'

Erin did. When she and Jenna had been going through IVF cycles it had almost become their identity and friends and family had seemed so apart from that. Telling themselves that it was best to stay in and rest, do nothing, after each embryo transfer, to give that embryo the best chance. They'd not answered phones, they'd done nothing except try to nurture Jenna and hope that the embryo implanted. Only emerging two weeks later each time with crushing defeat and grief in their hearts. She'd not felt that her own family had understood what she was going through. None of them had had trouble conceiving and so the distance between them all grew. It was only after her split with Jenna that she'd realised how much she'd missed the support of her family. How important it was for her to re-establish their connection and closeness.

'She lived with me and Brad for a while. We'd been married about three years, Hazel was eighteen and our parents emigrated and asked us to take her in, which we did. We were so close back then! She didn't want to go to university, but she got some NVQs and went into childcare and then became a teaching assistant in a primary school.'

NVQs were National Vocational Qualifications. 'She never wanted to be a teacher?'

Zoey laughed. 'Oh, no! She didn't fancy all that paperwork. I think she was with us for about three years before she moved out on her own and came to Westcombe.'

'She's at the local primary, then?'

She nodded. 'Yes. Anyway, sorry to butt in on your consultation, but I was worried about her when she mentioned the dizziness. I know how poorly she's been with the morning sickness.'

'Oh, not a problem, don't worry.'

'I'll let you get on.'

A part of Erin wanted Zoey to stay. To sit and chat. She liked sitting and listening to Zoey talk. She was often so animated. Eyes bright, gesturing. Smiling. Laughing. She liked that best of all, Zoey's laugh. '*Warms me cockles*,' as her dad used to say.

'I'll see you later.'

When Zoey left, it was as if all the oxygen was taken from the room. As if the light had faded. The warmth gone. Erin shook her head, telling herself she was being ridiculous for thinking in such a manner and got on with typing up some notes and then checking some blood results that had come in for other patients, whilst she waited for her next patient to arrive. They seemed to be a little late for their appointment. It happened sometimes, but she really hoped that this patient wouldn't be a no-show. Sometimes as a doctor, you got a sixth sense about somebody. That there might be something going on that they were not saying.

Rachel Dring didn't come to the surgery often for health problems. Hardly ever, in fact, but she did have to come in for her asthma reviews, and when she did, she brought her husband, Aiden, with her. Aiden was a large man. A good six feet in height, maybe more, and he had what Erin called a club bouncer's build. Clearly, the man went to the gym and worked out. But it was the way Rachel acted in her appointments that made Erin think there were red flags. She'd never said anything outright. Never shown up with bruises or any kind of physical injuries, but Erin always got the sense that the woman was scared of her husband. She'd asked Keiko about whether she should flag it to adult safeguarding. But as there was no visible evidence, nor had Rachel said anything herself and this was just based on Erin's feeling, they had decided to just keep an eye on things and put a note on her record for any practitioner to be alert for any signs of abuse.

Today, she was due in for another review and Erin kept checking the clock. If she was more than five minutes late then she would have to call in her next patient after Rachel, as they'd already arrived. And just as she was thinking of calling in that next patient, Rachel's name lit up on the system to let Erin know that she had checked in.

*Thank goodness!*

Barely giving her time to sit down, Erin called her through and, as anticipated, her husband, Aiden, followed her in, sitting down beside her.

'Hello Rachel. Aiden. How are you doing?'

Her patient looked like she always did. Pale-faced. Timid. Her hair was a little unkempt and needed a wash.

'I'm fine, Doctor.'

'Glad to hear it. So, you're here for your asthma review. How have you been getting along?'

Rachel smiled. 'Good. No problems, really.'

'How often are you having to use your inhalers?'

As she listened to Rachel speak, she couldn't help but take in and notice the small details. Rachel's nails bitten down to the quick. The dark circles beneath her eyes. The way she spoke. As if she was expecting to be interrupted by Aiden at any minute. Her *considered* answers. Never a problem. Never anything wrong.

'I see there's a new doctor at the practice. Angela her name is, isn't it?'

Erin blinked, then smiled, understanding that this might be the moment she'd been hoping for. Of course there was no one at the surgery called Angela. But there was an initiative where women who felt unsafe could *Ask for Angela.* It was mostly for pubs and clubs, but it worked here, too.

'That's right. You know her?'

Rachel glanced at Aiden, then away. 'I think I went to school with her.'

'I'm sure she'd love to say hello. Give me a minute and I'll see if she's free.' Erin stood.

Aiden's face clouded over. 'We haven't got time for a bloody reunion, Rach. Let's just do the review and go. We've got other stuff to do.'

'She's just next door. Won't take a moment,' said Erin, closing her door behind her, hoping that they would stay in the room as she hurried over to Zoey's door. Keiko was gone for the day and she didn't want to leave Rachel and Aiden alone for as long as she would need to head to Reception, so she knocked quickly on Zoey's door and didn't even wait for permission to go in. She just did.

Thankfully, Zoey was alone.

'Oh, hey. What's up?'

'My current patient has just asked for Angela. I don't think she's safe. Can you call the police for me?'

'Of course. Can you keep them talking? Is it safe for you to go back into the room?'

'I think so.'

'If you're not sure, you shouldn't go in there.'

'I can't leave her in there alone with her husband.'

Zoey picked up the phone and began to dial and Erin headed back to her room, feigning her apologies. 'I'm so sorry, but she's with a patient right now, so let's finish your review, shall we, and then you can get on.'

Rachel nodded and looked disappointed.

'It's time to go,' Aiden said.

'I just need to check her spirometry levels. Won't take more than a few minutes,' she explained, hoping it was enough to convince Aiden from walking his wife out of there.

'How long will that take?'

'A couple of minutes, that's all. You wouldn't want Rachel's asthma to get worse.'

He sighed. 'Fine.'

But she could tell that it wasn't fine. Not really.

He didn't like that he couldn't control Erin the way he controlled Rachel.

Erin pulled the spirometer from her supply cupboard, applied a mouthpiece and explained its use to Rachel. 'You know what this is, but I'll explain again. A spirometer measures how much air your lungs can hold, volume, flow, that kind of thing, and how much you can breathe out in one forced breath. I'm going to pop a nose clip on you, if that's okay?'

Rachel nodded and Erin took her time in applying it to her patient's nose, pretending it was all about comfort and making sure it wasn't pinching. Really, she was just stalling. Hopefully, the police would get here quickly.

'Okay, so you're going to sit upright for me. That's it. Shoulders relaxed and then you're going to take in the deepest breath that you can and exhale it into the mouthpiece as hard and as fast as you can. Got it?'

Another nod.

'It might make you cough, but you'll be okay.'

'All right.'

'We're going to do it three times.' She couldn't help but glance past them and out to the front of the building. She hoped that she would see the familiar outline of a police car in the car park, but there was nothing there yet. 'First try.'

Rachel inhaled a deep breath and then blew into the spirometer, before breaking into a coughing fit.

'You're okay. You're doing great. When you're ready, do the second one.' A movement in her peripheral vision out of the window. A police car on its way down the lane. *Thank goodness!* She was just waiting for Rachel to stop coughing after her second attempt when there was a knock at her door. 'Oh, that'll be Angela!' Erin took Rachel's hand and stood her up. 'Why not surprise her and answer the door yourself?' she said, escorting Rachel to the door.

'Wait—'

Rachel opened the door, not knowing what to expect.

Erin immediately saw the two police officers on the other side, Zoey standing behind them both, looking anxious.

Aiden stood and laughed. 'What's she done now?' he asked, trying to seem charming, yet also deflecting because of course they weren't here for him, were they? Make the police think that Rachel had done wrong immediately. That he was the innocent one.

'Rachel Dring?' asked the officer, the taller of the two.

'Yes?' Rachel asked querulously.

'Might we have a word?'

'What's going on? What's she done?' asked Aiden again, his smile starting to fail.

The other officer, male, broad-set and muscular, stepped forward to address him, almost in a conspiratorial way, as if he were on Aiden's side. 'If you'd come me with me sir, I can let you know what's going on. Rachel's safe, don't you worry.'

Aiden flashed a glance in Rachel's direction

but allowed himself to be taken away by the burly policeman.

Rachel, now alone, sagged in relief as Aiden was taken away to another room.

'Do you have somewhere we could talk to Rachel?' the other officer asked Erin.

She showed them another room they could use and the remaining officer disappeared with her in there. There was a small commotion from Aiden's room and then he was led out, arms behind his back, cursing and swearing in protest. The officer held something alarming in his hand. A weapon of some kind.

Later, in the small staff room, Erin and Zoey sat Rachel down. 'You did a brave thing today,' Erin said.

Rachel was shivering and shaking, tears welling in her eyes. 'What are they gonna do to him?'

'I don't know. But they'll certainly try and keep him away from you, that's for sure,' Zoey said. 'Let me get you a tea.'

Erin turned to Rachel. 'Are you hurt?'

She nodded and lifted up her top to show a slicing wound on her abdomen. 'He said he'd cut me for real and he did, because some guy said hello to me at the supermarket. Said I had embarrassed him by flirting with him, but I didn't!'

Erin frowned. 'Let's get that cleaned up. Have you had a tetanus injection lately?'

Rachel shrugged and began to cry. Erin draped an arm around her patient's shoulder and Zoey put Rachel's mug of tea down on the table in front of her and passed her a tissue for her tears.

'We'll keep you safe. Don't you worry about that.'

Later that evening after work, Zoey invited Erin round for tea at her cottage so that they could both decompress from the day that they'd had. After Aiden's arrest, they had helped get Rachel into a women's shelter over in the next town, after they'd accompanied her to her house to get her things. Her sister would come down from London as soon as she could to collect her and take her back with her. No one knew how long the police would hold Aiden, so once Rachel was settled they'd left and headed for home.

'What a day.'

Erin sipped at her tea and let out a contented sigh. 'I knew I was right to trust my instincts. I *knew* something was going on!'

'Thank goodness you interpreted her question about Angela the right way. Imagine if you hadn't known about it and had simply believed she was asking for someone at the practice called Angela.'

'It doesn't bear thinking about, does it? Imagine living in fear like that every day.'

Zoey nodded. 'She couldn't be herself. I bet she doesn't even know who she is any more. The parts that made her who she was slowly stripped away by her husband, piece by piece, until only a small bit of the real her is left.'

'She'll find her way. It'll take time, but I think with the right support and as long as she doesn't go back to him, then she can be who she was always meant to be.'

'I think she'll do it. She was brave enough to take a step today, with him right by her side. I think without him, once she's healed and got stronger, she'll have even more courage to live authentically.'

Erin took another sip. 'Do you think it happens in every relationship?'

'What?'

'That when you're with someone, even if they love you and you love them and there's no threat of violence and even in a happy, balanced relationship…do you think you lose parts of yourself?'

Such a deep question. Zoey could only think about it in terms of her own experience with Brad. There'd been no abuse. She had never feared him. Their relationship had been calm and sedate.

'I don't know. Maybe? I was with Brad for fifteen years and I know I changed to fit in with the kind of life we shared. I made parts of myself smaller sometimes so that he could shine.' In particular, she thought of some of the dinners they'd attended and how she'd let Brad do the talking, whilst she'd simply stood by his side. Or the family celebrations at his parents' house. There, Brad was the star. He was primary. She was secondary. She'd never really told anyone that. Or thought about it. She'd just accepted the relationship for what it was without demanding more, even when there were times when she'd needed it.

'But surely you shone as well. An accomplished woman. Clever. Working.'

She shrugged. Was she really sharing the details of her marriage with Erin? They'd only known each other a week. 'We had a decent life. I never wanted to muddy the waters or cause a storm.'

'Asking for what you need from your partner should never cause a storm.'

Zoey nodded. She knew Erin was right. If someone loved you, truly loved you, then they should at least listen if you sat them down and asked for a chat about things. About changing something up. About adapting. 'I know. I just didn't want to rock the boat.'

'That's a lot of sailing metaphors.' Erin smiled at her.

She laughed. 'We live in a fishing village. What can I say? I'm influenced by my surroundings.'

She paused for a moment though, thinking about it. It was nice sitting here in the cottage with Erin, just chatting. They'd done something good today that had really helped someone. They might even have saved a life and they'd done it together. And here they sat, amongst unpacked boxes still, sharing a cup of tea and companionship and it felt really nice. And she didn't want it to end.

'Do you want to stay for dinner? I think I've got some pasta in there which should be more than enough.'

Erin smiled. 'I'd love to.'

It had intrigued Erin, hearing a little about what Zoey's marriage had been like. Fascinating, actually. The Zoey she had come to know over this past week was wonderful. Interesting. Admirable. And yet when she spoke of time spent with her husband, Brad, she'd admitted that she had made herself smaller and said they'd had a decent life.

Was making yourself smaller so someone else could shine how Erin would define a decent relationship? No. Absolutely not! And who would want to hear that their relationship with someone was decent?

Not her, anyway. The word conjured up an image of a relationship that was okay enough. With no particular highlights. A few lows, that they might crawl out of. Livable.

It made Erin feel hurt on Zoey's behalf. Someone like Zoey deserved so much better! Joy and happiness. Times that could be amazing and fill her heart with wonder, delight and elation. Exhilaration! Had Zoey ever had a moment like that with Brad?

She didn't ask, not wanting to seem like she was picking holes in someone's relationship. Zoey must have loved her husband. She was with him for fifteen years; there must have been something that made her stay. And so instead, she helped Zoey prepare dinner, chopping tomatoes and courgettes for a pasta sauce, whilst Zoey grated some cheese as the pasta simmered on the stove.

'Garlic bread?' Zoey asked.

'Ooh, yes, please.'

When it was done, they headed into what would eventually be Zoey's living room and sat down together on a two-seater couch to eat their meal. It was simple and rustic, but hit the spot. It had been a long day. Zoey turned on the television and found a movie channel and stuck on a romcom. And with a glass of wine each, they settled in for the evening to watch it.

Erin could have stayed like that forever. But soon the movie was over and it was getting late and if she didn't get back soon, her cat Pixie would stage a protest over her empty food bowl.

'Well, I guess I ought to get going. Thank you for dinner.'

Zoey yawned and smiled. 'You're very welcome.'

'My turn next, okay?'

'Deal.'

They walked to the front door, Erin wishing she could drag her feet and stay a bit longer but she had taken up enough of Zoey's time today, ever since she'd involved her in Rachel's case.

'I hope I didn't interrupt any plans you had for this evening.'

'Are you kidding me? All I had planned was a long evening unpacking boxes.'

'You should have said. I could have helped.'

Zoey shrugged. 'It's fine. Dinner and a movie were much better. We should do this again some time.'

Erin smiled. 'I'd like that. But like I said, I'll cook next time and you can be my guest.'

'I'll look forward to it.'

'Okay.' Erin leaned in to give her a goodbye

hug. It seemed like the kind of thing good friends would do and she sensed that Zoey was a hugger, but as soon as she wrapped her arms around Zoey and she wrapped her arms around her, an awareness, a need, a desire, spread through her. An image of the two of them kissing. It turning hot, them slamming the door closed and kissing and stumbling their way to the bedroom…

Erin let go and stepped back as if Zoey was molten rock and she'd been burned by her touch. Face colouring, she forced a smile and a weird little wave and stepped out into the fresh air.

She hurried down the garden path and only when she heard Zoey's door close did she let out a breath and thank her lucky stars that she'd had the wherewithal to step away.

*Note to self—don't hug Zoey ever again!*

# CHAPTER FIVE

'HEDRA JAMESON?' ERIN SMILED as her patient got up from her chair in the waiting room and waited for her to enter her consulting room and closed the door. 'Morning, Miss Jameson, how can I help you today?'

Hedra was her last clinic patient of the morning. She'd already seen and diagnosed a patient with a urinary tract infection, another with a possible slipped disc, one with tennis elbow, two different patients with migraines and had had to call an ambulance out for a COPD patient with bad oxygen levels. Zoey had taken a couple of her patients for her whilst she'd dealt with the emergency and now her last patient was Hedra.

There wasn't much in her history. She didn't seem to come to the doctors' often. But when the booking had been made, the note from the team on Reception had been two simple words—mental health.

Hedra settled herself into the chair next to Erin's desk. 'I'm struggling.'

'Okay. Why don't you tell me more about that?'

Hedra placed her bag on the floor, folded her hands neatly on her lap. 'I don't know how to describe it, actually. I just feel like I'm failing at life in all areas. Work. Home. Relationships. I think… I might be depressed.'

'And how long have you been feeling this way?'

She could see that Hedra was trying to fight back tears and so she passed over the tissue box, just in case.

'My partner, Eddie, he left me a couple of months ago and it's kind of been downhill ever since. He found someone else, tale as old as time.' She tried to laugh and dabbed at her eyes with a tissue. 'But he's left me with a house I can't afford, so I've had to put it up for sale, and my boss at work has told me that because the business doesn't do so well as we go into winter, he wants to cut my hours from forty to twelve per week, which of course means less money and I'm going to need to find another job. I've stopped seeing my friends because I can't afford to go out and socialise with them any more and I just want to hide under my duvet every day and I have no desire to do anything!'

The tears fell properly then and as Hedra sobbed, Erin tried to think of what to do. Her patient had so many issues going on that she couldn't fix—the ex, the house, the job, the money. But what she could do was support Hedra with her mental health.

'Are you sleeping?'

Hedra nodded. 'Too much.'

'Okay. Do you have family close?'

'My mum lives in Eastcombe.' The next town over. It didn't sit on the coast the way Westcombe did. It was further inland.

'Well, I can understand why you've been feeling overwhelmed. It probably feels right now that you're being hit left, right and centre.'

Erin knew the feeling. She'd bought a flat with Jenna over in West Sussex. They'd bought it together, created a home, imagined a future. When it all fell apart and Jenna moved out, Erin was left trying to meet a mortgage she couldn't afford on her own. Jenna had needed her to sell up, so she could get her half of the money back, effectively making Erin homeless from a place she'd loved. Then, to add insult to injury, she'd kept seeing Jenna out and about with her new beau—the ex-boyfriend who had finally got Jenna pregnant—and each time it had felt like a stab to the heart and so she'd known she had to get out of the area, too. Unable to face the idea of running into them in a few months' time as a family, pushing a stroller and looking into the face of a baby that should have been theirs. When your life imploded the only thing you could do was look for security. Something that made you feel safe. And so she'd come to Westcombe. Initially for a long locum contract that had become permanent and now she had a lovely cottage here. Was happy here. Things could work out, but only if you put the work in to make it that way.

'Have you thought about talking to someone?'

'I'm talking to you!'

'And that's great. It's a good first step. But I was thinking of someone who could give you more time than the ten minutes we're allotted. I was thinking of a counsellor or therapist.'

'I can't afford that!'

'Well, actually, there's a free talking service you can access here. I can give you the details and you don't need a referral from me; you can access it yourself.' Erin pulled a leaflet from her desk drawer and slid it over to Hedra. 'Give them a call if you think it will help. They could help you out in many different ways. Also, there's the choice of taking medication if you feel that would help, but if you do want to go down that route, just be aware that it can take a few weeks before you'd feel any benefit.'

'I don't want that. Talking to someone sounds good though.'

'So you're going to contact the service?'

Hedra nodded and managed a smile.

'I'd also like to suggest that instead of hiding under the duvet, you try and get out and about. Go for a walk. Get some fresh air. Being outside and walking has proven highly beneficial to people suffering with depression.'

'I can do that. We have—I have—a small dog. I've been letting his walks slide.'

'Perfect. It's even been proven that stroking the fur of a beloved pet also shows benefits to humans. So, talking therapies, eight hours sleep and no more, fresh air, exercise and walking your dog, yes?'

Hedra let out a breath. 'Yes.'

'You know, we also have a social advisor here at the practice. They can help and advise on non-medical issues such as jobs and housing. Would you like to talk to them to see if they can help you arrange something? Make you feel a little less alone as you navigate these changes?'

'That would be great, thank you.'

Erin grabbed the referral slip and signed it. 'Take this to Reception and ask them to make an appointment for you.'

'I will. Thank you, Doctor.' Hedra stood to go.

'You've taken a huge positive step today. You should feel proud. You're going to get through this, but just know that you need to keep talking to people. Share your issues. I think you'll find that those near and dear to you will want to help if they can. And if you have any other issues, or you feel the depression is getting worse, you can always come back and see me. Will you book an appointment to see me in a few weeks' time to see how you're getting on? It can be a telephone appointment or face to face.'

'I'll do that. Thank you.'

'My pleasure.'

When Hedra was gone, Erin hoped most dearly that she had helped in some way. Opened avenues to help, anyway, that Hedra could access. When she'd entered Erin's room, the world had looked dark, but hopefully now her patient felt as if she had a way forward through the mess and that she wouldn't be going through it alone, the way Erin had felt like she did when her world had come crashing down around her ears.

*I wonder what Jenna is doing right now?*

*Is she happy with the choices she made?*

She had to be. She had everything that she and Erin had ever wanted. A child of their own. A family. And she'd left Erin to achieve it. Jenna had to be ecstatic!

It hurt though, to feel that she'd been superfluous. Jenna should have turned to her. To Erin. They'd both been going through the hell of failed IVF cycles. Every negative test had been a heavy blow. A sucker punch to them both. And each time they had both grieved for the baby they never had. That they'd hoped for. Imagined. Dreamed of. Instead, Jenna had turned from her and into the arms of her ex and got pregnant that way.

It had been a double insult. To lose the woman she loved and the future family she'd dreamed of. To lose the home they had created so beautifully. Because Erin couldn't give Jenna what she'd craved most of all.

She'd not been enough.

She'd been discarded. Like rubbish. Useless. Throwaway. Not needed.

And she vowed to never feel that way ever again.

It had been a long day and Zoey was tired. She was looking forward to getting home, having something to eat and then a long soak in the bath whilst she read her book. It was all she wanted to do. She could even imagine in that moment the bubbles in the bath, her painted toenails peeking out of the water. A nice glass of white wine, dripping with condensation as she sipped from it. Perfect! And then…

'Somebody help! I need help!'

Zoey had been standing by the door, about to drape her bag over her shoulder and head for home. Instead, she yanked her door open and went running down to Reception, mere milliseconds behind Erin.

A young lad stood there, panting, face sweaty and red, hair damp. 'It's my dad! He's had a fall!'

'Is he outside?' Erin asked, heading back to the utility room to grab the emergency bag.

The boy shook his head. 'He fell over the harbour wall and landed on some rocks!'

Zoey swallowed. That sounded like it could be bad. 'Has anyone called 999?'

'She's trying, but there's no signal down by the harbour.'

'Let's go! I've got my keys,' Erin said, rushing past them both and grabbing the boy's arm. 'You come with us too. Direct us to where your dad is. Did you run here?'

They got in the car and Zoey dialled for the emergency services as they sped off down the lane that would take them to the harbour. It was in walking distance, but in an emergency like this one every second could count and they arrived at the harbour in less than a minute. They could see a crowd had gathered, people looking shocked, their lovely day at the seaside ending with the sight of a man who could be badly injured.

'What's your dad's name?' Erin asked the boy.

'Lee.'

Zoey's tiredness had evaporated as adrenaline flooded her system. She'd not attended an emergency case such as this since she'd been a foundation doctor working in Accident and Emergency, a rotation that she'd absolutely hated. There was just something about the atmosphere of an emergency that made her feel sick. One wrong move, one wrong decision could have catastrophic repercussions for the patient. It was why she preferred being a GP. The cases weren't usually life and death in that very moment. Her job allowed her the benefit of time. Of trying different solutions until they found the right one that would work for that individual. Sometimes, all that was needed from her was the need to listen.

Zoey and Erin and the boy leapt from the car and pushed their way through the assembled throng and looked over the harbour wall to the rocks below that would normally be covered by the sea. But right now, the tide was out and it was quickly coming in. Time was not on their side, or on the patient's side. A man, the boy's father, lying on the rocks below, unconscious, looking for all the world like a broken toy. One leg bent in a way that it should never bend and, worst of all, a trickle of blood coming out from behind the man's head. Beside him, holding his hand, a woman. Presumably his wife, the boy's mother.

'The steps!' Erin pointed and they rushed over to them.

At the top they looked clean enough, but as they got further down and reached the waterline they looked a little more dangerous. Covered in limpets and dark green seaweed that could cause them to slip if they weren't careful.

*Before you go rushing in, make sure it is safe.*

'Watch your step,' she told Erin, who had flung off her heels and in stockinged feet begun to descend first, the straps of the emergency bag over each shoulder like a backpack.

Zoey followed, her heart hammering in her chest. Whatever they did next would be crucial. Whatever they did next could determine if this man lived and if he lived without problems. She could feel the eyes of everyone up on the harbour wall watching them. A glance up and she saw some of those people had got their phones out, recording the scenario. It made her feel sick. Made her want to scream at them.

*Don't you see this man's hurt?*

*Give him some dignity!*

Would they share it on social media later? Show their friends? Their families? Why would they do that? She pushed the invasive thoughts away and jumped down to the mix of sand and stone that waited at the bottom of the steps with Erin and then they set off across the pebbles and stones towards the larger rocky area where the man lay, bleeding and broken.

'I'll primary survey,' Erin said as they stumbled over the larger stones towards the rocks. 'You get the collar out, the oxygen and whatever else you think we'll need.'

Zoey nodded as she began to carefully clamber over the large rocks they had to climb to get to the man at the foot of the harbour wall. Thankfully, the large boulders were solidly in situ. These things were not going to move ever, but still she was careful. It would be oh, so easy to slip on some of the algae and seaweed that clung to some of them and fall into the gaps in between.

Erin reached him first. 'Lee? Lee, can you hear me?' She placed a hand either side of his face and tried to look in the man's eyes as Zoey reached the last rock and pulled the bag from Erin's back and lay it on the rock, unzipping it to expose the abundance of medical equipment inside. She grabbed the cervical collar.

'Here. Get this on him,' she said.

Erin grabbed it and slowly wrapped it around Lee's neck. When her hands came away, they were bloodied from a wound on the back of his head.

Zoey passed her gloves and put on her own, then she attached the adult rebreather mask to the oxygen tank and turned it on full and placed the mask over Lee's face. She was aware of Erin slowly assessing Lee's form.

'Depressed skull fracture…no fluid or bleeding from ears…'

Zoey passed over the pen light.

Erin shone it into his eyes. 'Unequal pupils.'

*Damn. That's not a good sign.*

'Can you get the BP cuff? Pelvis feels normal, but obvious open fracture of the right tibia and fibia…'

Zoey passed over the cuff, then grabbed the stethoscope and began to listen to Lee's chest. It was hard to hear over the noise around them, but there were definitely no sounds of inflation coming from the right lung. 'Right pneumothorax.' She looked up and met Erin's eyes. There wasn't the equipment in the kitbag to do a needle decompression. Or to place a chest tube. She felt helpless. Despondent. Even a little panicked.

The sound of sirens could be heard but, even better than that, the sound of a helicopter approaching. *Please be the air ambulance!* If it was, an emergency doctor would be onboard and they could help this man better than she and Erin could and airlift him to a hospital more quickly than he could get to one by road. The nearest hospital was a good hour away; it would be minutes by helicopter and she and Erin had no idea of what damage the depressed skull fracture was causing, or what was happening with the collapsed lung.

Lee groaned and tried to move, but Zoey was there and laid her hands upon his chest. 'Stay where you are, Lee. Help is coming. You need to stay still.' His eyes rolled back and he lost consciousness again and Zoey looked up into Erin's eyes. This was why she'd hated being in Accident and Emergency. The feeling that you could lose someone and there was nothing you could do about it.

Like with Brad. The cardiac arrest had not happened at work; it had been at home. It had been a beautiful day, much like this one, the sun shining, the sky clear of clouds. She and Brad had been in the garden. Zoey had been reading a book in the shade of the greengage tree. Her husband had been digging out a rose they'd wanted to move to a different location, but its root system was vast and he was having trouble digging it out when suddenly he'd straightened and made a noise.

*'Bad back again?'*

*'No, it's my shoulder, it feels like...'*

He'd never got to finish his sentence. In fact, Brad had never said another word ever again. They were his last words. And he'd dropped like a stone. Zoey had rushed over to him so fast, tried to shake him awake, but like Lee, his eyes had rolled into the back of his head and he'd stopped breathing.

She'd never felt so helpless.

Never felt so incompetent as a doctor.

Of course, she'd started chest compressions and had begun yelling for help. A neighbour had been in their garden too and had peered over the fence, seen what was happening and dialled the emergency services, but it was too late. A post-mortem had revealed that Brad had suffered a sudden cardiac arrest and that he'd probably been dead before he'd even hit the ground. But Zoey would never forget those moments trying to bring him back—performing CPR without the help of oxygen or a defibrillator—and when the paramedics had finally arrived, one of them had led her away and made her a cup of tea and she'd sat in her living room in a state of shock, hands trembling, unable to believe what had just happened.

She was snapped back into the present by the arrival of the helicopter, the downdraught from the whizzing blades making her and Erin cover Lee to protect him from any debris that might be caught up in the force.

Where would they land? The tide was incoming. They couldn't land on the beach; there was no time! But now there were flashing blue lights at the harbour wall and an ambulance had arrived too and paramedics were making their way down the steps to help them. Zoey began shouting details of the patient's condition to them as they clambered over the stones and boulders so they would know what to do the second they got to Lee.

When they did, Erin and Zoey helped apply the splint to Lee's leg. Clearly, he was out of it as he didn't even moan. Then Erin was able to use the paramedics' equipment to access a vein for an intravenous line.

'We need to get him off these rocks and onto a spinal board,' Erin said. 'Now we've got enough people, I'll take the head, you guys grab his body and legs. Zoey, you guide us off these rocks and wait for us at the bottom.'

Zoey scrambled away.

'We're gonna lift him on three, okay. One, two, three!'

Zoey watched them hoist Lee easily, but now it was the matter of telling them which was going to be the smoothest path off the rocks. Step by step, she guided them, avoiding the boulders with anything on that could make them slip. Letting them know where the gaps were, making sure they kept Lee safe all the way down to the pebbles and sand at the base of the rocks. The water was very close now, but thankfully, the helicopter crew arrived, including an emergency doctor. Erin and Zoey gave her the details of the accident and what exams and treatment they had given. Then the paramedics got her up-to-date on what they'd done. Together, they all hoisted Lee back up and began to walk. There was a corner they all needed to get around and they were all going to get their feet wet, but they'd make it to the beach okay.

As predicted, there were one or two sticky moments where their feet sank into the sand beneath the incoming tide, a couple of wobbles as boots got stuck, but everyone waited until that person was able to pull free and get back onto solid ground and then they began marching up the beach.

The onlookers began to clap and then a woman and the young boy who had initially fetched them from the surgery came running up. 'Is he okay? Lee? Lee, can you hear me?'

The emergency doctor informed Lee's wife which hospital they'd be taking her husband to and that she'd have to drive, as there was no room on the helicopter for passengers.

There was a football field at the community centre where the helicopter had landed and Erin and Zoey walked with the crew all the way to the air ambulance and stood back as it lifted up into the air and flew away with their patient.

They were left standing there, bewildered and

amazed, windswept and hot, watching the helicopter disappear into the distance. Then they turned to look at one another.

'Well, I wasn't expecting that!' Zoey said, laughing, as a release of adrenaline surged through her body. She felt exhilarated, excited and exhausted.

'Nor me.' Erin smoothed her hair and somehow, miraculously, seemed to be well put together again in an instant, even sans shoes. 'We make a great team, don't we?'

Zoey looked at her. Thought *My goodness, she's beautiful* and then nodded. 'We do.' Feeling her mouth go dry, her heart pitter-patter. A longing so strong to just step forward and sweep Erin into her arms and just hold her close. Breathe her in. Soak in the wonder that was Dr Erin Bramley.

'We ought to go back to the surgery and write that incident up.'

*That was sensible*, Zoey thought. *More sensible than my initial reaction.*

'We need to find your shoes.'

Erin looked down at her now dirty feet. 'Hmm. Yeah.'

'And then it's my shout. You must come and have dinner with me. My treat. I think we both deserve it.'

'You want to cook for me again?'

'Actually, I was thinking more about going out to eat someplace. The Seagull pub does some great food by all accounts and we could even do the pub quiz. The two of us with our heads together should be able to answer most questions, I think.'

Erin nodded. 'Sounds perfect.'

It was such a lovely evening, the intense heat of the day gone, that they decided to walk down into the village and on to the pub. On the way down, Erin showed Zoey some of her favourite viewing spots of the bay and she did try to enjoy them as she usually did, but it was difficult with Zoey at her side.

When she'd knocked on her door earlier, Zoey had answered wearing a beautiful yet simple dress that had taken Erin's breath away. A spaghetti strap pale blue sundress that enhanced the blue of Zoey's eyes and with her white blonde hair made her look like some sort of summer snow queen. She wore a dainty silver necklace with a teardrop pendant that kept reflecting the sun and she looked so fresh-faced and so innocent and fragile it was hard to believe that this was the same woman who had clambered over jagged rocks with her just an hour or so ago. The dress narrowed at her waist and flared out again into a full, floaty skirt, revealing shapely calves, and on her feet she wore bright white flats that looked brand-new.

'You look nice,' she'd said and then wanted to kick herself for saying something so inane. *Nice?* Zoey looked *stunning.*

'Thanks. So do you.'

Erin wasn't so sure about that. She'd put on a pale pink linen shirt and some white fitted shorts. An outfit that she had struggled with ever since she'd stepped inside her cottage. At work, she wore a lot of smart, formal clothes. So when she wasn't at work she liked to kick back and relax. But would she be relaxing this evening with Zoey?

The walk down to the village was strange. They would be walking, happily chatting side by side, and then their hands would occasionally accidentally brush against the other and Erin would pull her hand away, as if shocked, and move further away from Zoey and then she'd forget she was trying to keep her distance as they talked and laughed and, before she knew it, their hands, their fingertips, would brush each other's again. Did Zoey notice how it was making her feel? Erin hoped not. She'd hate to scare her off, or make her feel uncomfortable. But deep down, a part of her sensed that Zoey felt very comfortable in the company of women.

The Seagull pub was situated just off the seafront, but what Erin liked about it was its large gardens. Whoever had landscaped them knew what they were doing. Flowers and blooms overflowed everywhere and where the grassy area ended and the cliff began, they had used the cliffside to grow heathers and luxuriant mosses. There was a small pavilion, lit by lanterns and shaded by an ancient grapevine whose tendrils explored everywhere and it was there that they sat, in the shade, whilst they dined on shrimp starters, monkfish wrapped in prosciutto, served with a warm brown butter sauce and pea puree and decadent frosted chocolate truffles served on a bed of hazelnut mousse and blackcurrant coulis.

'It's official. I'm never moving from this spot,' laughed Zoey as she dabbed at her lips with a napkin and beamed at Erin over the table.

There was a candle on their table and even though it was still daylight, the shade from the vine and the lit candle reflected light and dancing shadows across Zoey's face. Her eyes sparkled with life and happiness and it made Erin feel very good to know that she had helped make her feel that way after the drama of their day.

'I don't see why we couldn't do our consults from here. Out in the open air. It might be nice,' she said with a smile.

'Mm. We'd only be able to consult though.

No examinations. We'd have to send everyone to the practice if they wanted to be checked over and then we'd have to schlep back and forth...'

'I guess there wouldn't be much confidentiality either. The Seagull's staff might overhear as they're laying out the tables.'

'True.' Zoey chuckled then and it was so delightful it made Erin *beam*. 'Thank you for dinner, Erin. This was so nice after such a dramatic day.'

'Thank you for joining me. You made the evening much nicer than it would have been if I'd come here alone.'

Was Zoey blushing? Was that flush of colour that swept so beautifully across her face caused by Erin's words?

'Do you often eat out alone?'

'Sometimes. But I don't really enjoy it. It's better with company.'

'I've never done it. I was always with Brad. Every year we'd go into London on our wedding anniversary, see a show, have a meal after, stay in a hotel for the night and then go home. I can't imagine doing that by myself.'

'You must miss him?' The question was out of her mouth before she'd even thought about whether she should ask it.

Zoey sighed and looked off into the distance, thinking about it. 'The dutiful wife part of me feels like I should say *Of course* straight away. He was part of my life for fifteen years and he was a good friend. A good companion. Easy to talk to, if nothing else. So, if you're asking me if I miss my friend, then yes, I do. You'd think me awful if I ever said anything else.'

What could she mean? Erin leaned forward, her hand playing with the stem of her wineglass. 'I could never think of you as awful. Ever.'

Zoey gave a short grateful smile. 'My marriage to Brad was quiet. Unassuming. There were never fireworks. There were never moments of excitement or high-octane thrills. He made me feel safe. He made me feel like I never had to worry about him.'

Erin wasn't sure what to say. 'You weren't lonely, but you almost sound alone.' And she reached out, placed a reassuring hand on Zoey's and held her fingers within her grip. Brad might not have instilled excitement or fireworks in Zoey's life, but this woman opposite was certainly making her feel like they were there. Her heart *pounded* in her chest. And butterflies danced merrily in her stomach, drunk on white wine and truffles.

Zoey seemed to look down at their entwined hands; her lips parted as her breath hitched in her throat.

Would she pull her hand away? *Have I over-*

*stepped the mark? What on earth am I doing holding onto her hand?*

Erin was going to release her to make it less awkward, but suddenly Zoey was squeezing her fingers *back*.

'I was so lonely! But I told no one. Not even Hazel.'

Zoey's voice trembled a little and she pressed her lips together as she gathered herself and took a deep breath. 'I thought for a long time that there was something wrong with me. What reason did I have to complain? Here I was, married to a lovely man, another doctor, from a good family, living in a fine house, with no money worries, no trust issues, no worries that my husband might have an affair, and yet I felt like the life I was living was *not mine*. Like I was looking at the rest of the world as if through a fishbowl.'

'You felt trapped.'

Zoey nodded. 'Yes!'

She would have said more, Erin had no doubt, but in that moment Zoey's mobile rang and for a second Erin thought that Zoey might ignore it, but the insistent ringing finally caused her to let go of Erin's hand and fish in her bag for her phone. 'It could be Hazel,' she said. 'I'd better answer.'

Erin sat back, looking down at the hand that

Zoey had held. It felt as if she could still feel her touch. A ghostly memory playing across her skin.

Then Zoey was sighing, 'Brad's mother,' as she looked at the screen. 'I'd better answer or she'll keep ringing.' She pressed her finger to the screen. 'Hello?'

Serena's concerned voice filled her ear. 'Zoey! At last. We've not heard from you for a whole week!'

'Oh. Sorry about that. But you know how it is when you move. You need time to settle in and acclimatize. New job. New home. New colleagues.' At this last one, she looked over at Erin. A moment ago, they'd been holding each other's hand and it had felt *wonderful*. Erin had made her feel seen. And she'd spilled a truth about her marriage that no one else had ever heard or managed to pull from her. Or if they had, they hadn't listened. Hadn't heard the need in her voice for more. But Erin had. She truly cared. Sign of a true friend? Or something else?

'Well, no, actually, I don't. I've lived in this house for ever, it seems. We miss you. Miss hearing your voice. We've been worried about you.'

'Well, I'm fine. To be honest with you, I'm better than fine! It's been good for me, the move.'

'Oh, you don't have to be brave for our sakes,

Zoey. We know you must feel terribly alone. Have you seen much of Hazel?'

'A couple of times.'

'So you were able to make time for your sister, but not make a quick phone call to us?'

Zoey bit down on her answer and said nothing. How did Serena always manage to turn words that sounded like concern into something that became accusative?

'You mustn't forget us, darling. We're *family* and always will be. Now, speaking of family and family time, Brad's birthday is coming up in a few weeks and we just want to confirm that you'll be coming as usual. Geoffrey needs to order the salmon.'

'Erm…'

'*It's tradition*, Zoey. You always come to ours on Brad's birthday. I cook his favourite foods, we honour his memory and we watch some old home videos. Geoffrey went up into the loft the other week and found some that we don't think you've seen yet. So, shall we say six o'clock?'

Serena always did this. Steamrollered any opposition to get what she wanted and needed to keep her son's memory alive. For two years, she had gone to theirs on Brad's birthday, even though she hadn't wanted to, because Serena would get weepy if Zoey said she might be busy. They expected twice weekly phone calls,

Wednesdays and Sundays. And Serena would always somehow mention that she'd been to the grave and how she'd not noticed any fresh flowers from her son's wife. How puzzled she'd be. '*Maybe the groundskeeper took them away?*'

But Zoey had moved away from Guildford. She was in Westcombe now, starting a new life, and she needed to let go of her old one if she were to move onto something new. She needed to make a firm stand now.

'I'm sorry, Serena, but I won't be coming.' She met Erin's gaze and mouthed *I'm sorry.*

There was a pause. A moment of silence that lasted so long she began to wonder if they had, in fact, been cut off.

'What do you mean, you're not coming? You always come. It's *tradition*.'

'I know, but…not any more. Not for me. You and Geoffrey can still celebrate in that way, but I'm busy here. I still haven't unpacked everything, I have a full-time job that takes up all of my time, and in the evenings I just want to rest.' She hoped Serena would understand.

'I can't believe you're abandoning us. Abandoning honouring your husband of fifteen years! You can let him go so easily?'

'I have to, Serena. There is no point in life of holding onto ghosts. It does no one any good.'

Another pause. 'I never thought you would

let us down like this, Zoey. When you said you were going to move, I told you it wasn't right for you and now it's proving to be true. It's changing you. Changing who you are.'

'That's right and I need that change. To finally be me.'

A sigh. She could imagine Serena's face.

'I'm hurt, Zoey. Very hurt! And the fact that you could discard Brad so easily!' Serena began to cry, but whether they were real tears or crocodile ones, Zoey couldn't know. But she did feel horrible. She felt incredibly guilty. But she'd needed to escape Guildford. Needed to escape the confines of Serena's grip on her and her insistence that Brad's memory be kept alive.

He was gone and nothing would bring him back. No yearly dinners. No watching hours of home footage of Brad as a little boy. No laying the freshest and most expensive flowers on his grave.

'I need to breathe and here I can do that, and I need you to accept it, even if you can't understand why you should.'

'I always had my doubts about you, you know. When Brad first introduced you to us, I said to Geoffrey, "One day that woman will break his heart!"'

'He's gone, Serena. His heart broke on its own, from an undiagnosed heart condition that he'd been born with. I gave him the best years of my life, but I have to live what is left of them for me and not for him.'

'What about Christmas? Will you come back at Christmas?'

Zoey closed her eyes. 'No. I'll be having Christmas in my own home. Making new traditions. New memories.'

The call ended. Serena had hung up. Unable to guilt trip Zoey into coming back, she had resorted to the only weapon she had left. Silence.

Blinking back tears, Zoey placed her phone back into her bag and sucked in a big breath before she could look at Erin through tear-filled eyes.

And suddenly Erin was on her feet and was pulling Zoey up onto hers and then throwing her arms around her and Zoey held on tight and cried into Erin's shoulder.

It felt so good to be held. So comforting to feel that she wasn't alone whilst she was hurting. Had she been wrong to say no to Serena? She didn't think so. Brad's parents had been stifling her for the last two years of her life! Their only connection to their son, they had held onto her and never wanted to let go. When they'd learned that she'd wanted to get rid of Brad's clothes to a charity shop, they'd been appalled. When they'd discovered that she'd wanted to get rid of the old bike he'd been restoring in the garage, they'd been in utter shock.

*'But he made that with his bare hands!'*

*'He put his heart and soul into that bike!'*

*'You can't just throw him away like that, Zoey!'*

It had been the same when she'd sorted through photo albums. When she'd tried to get rid of some of the things that Brad had bought for their home but she had never liked, Serena and Geoffrey would swoop in and take them for themselves, Serena looking at Zoey as if she was crazy.

She'd not been able to do anything, it seemed, without running it past her in-laws first. So when she'd put the house on the market…that was the first time Serena had hung up on her and stupidly, frantically, Zoey had called her back to try to explain even more, not wanting there to be conflict between her and them, and Serena had used that to manipulate.

'I just… I have to be able to live my life!' Zoey whispered into Erin's pink shirt that was becoming sodden beneath her tears.

'Of course you do,' Erin replied, hands smoothing down Zoey's back. 'It's not your fault.'

'She only ever thinks of herself!'

Erin nodded.

Zoey pulled back to look at her. 'Do you think

I'm being selfish? Not going back to celebrate my dead husband's birthday.'

Erin looked back at her and took Zoey's hands in hers. 'I want you to listen to me. You are the bravest woman I know. Starting again, after your life has imploded. Don't ever feel guilty for thinking of yourself after you've spent a lifetime fulfilling everyone else's needs. It's your time now and you should be allowed to live it however you see fit.'

Zoey nodded. Erin was right.

Erin was also beautiful and standing so close and holding both of her hands and…*people are looking.*

Zoey sniffed, nodded, laughed and let go. She'd just made a scene in a pub garden and made herself and Erin the focus of attention. 'We should go.'

'Sure. But we'd better pay first. Don't want to end the night at the police station.'

The walk back to the cottages was peaceful. Serene. Walking through the quiet lanes, admiring gardens and cottages and enjoying the view as they rose higher and higher.

But inside her head and her heart, Erin felt so conflicted. Brad's mother had just treated Zoey so appallingly, expecting her to go running back to Guildford because she had declared it. The way that woman had made Zoey feel… Did they not see what a beautiful, kind, warm-hearted and loving person Zoey was? Did they not see how she felt things so keenly? The death of her husband was a wound she kept trying to heal, but Brad's mother kept pulling it back open and making her bleed again.

She felt a strong protective instinct for Zoey. If she knew Brad's mother's number she'd phone it herself and give the other woman what for. For Erin knew all about how it felt to have your pain worsened when you were trying to get over a loss. Seeing Jenna out and about with her new beau. Thinking she was fine and then hearing the baby had been born and that Jenna would be a mother and Erin wasn't. Ripping open the stitches time and time again made the wound worse. Increased the scarring. Stopped you from being able to heal and leaving you open to be hurt even more.

And yet…though she felt keenly protective over Zoey, she also felt strangely aware of just how much she'd wanted to keep holding her in that beer garden at The Seagull. The press of her body against hers. How soft her hair was when she stroked it. The dizzying scent of her. Gentle. Floral. Light.

Maybe it was because it had been so long since she'd experienced physical touch from another woman? Maybe she was only responding because it had been so long? Maybe it was nothing to do with Zoey at all!

But she had to admit to herself, deep down inside, that she knew she was attracted to Zoey and that her feelings towards her grew with every moment they spent together. It was impossible not to. Zoey made her smile and laugh. Erin loved how thoughtful she was towards others and she seemed to have so much love to give.

It was terrifying to feel herself falling for Zoey. She'd only known her a week and she didn't think it was a silly crush. There was something about her. Maybe because she was unavailable? A work colleague. A grieving widow, who'd been married to a man.

That couldn't be her whole story. Erin knew instinctively if another woman looked at her in a certain way, and she'd caught a few looks that Zoey had cast in her direction. There was something there. But what?

Was she reading too much into this? She'd hate to overstep the mark and get this wrong, because she had to work with this woman and she liked it here in Westcombe. She didn't want to have her life be screwed up again and have to leave. She hated running. She hated feeling as if she'd been ousted from her last place.

'Thank you for this evening,' Zoey said as

they reached her cottage gate. It creaked as she swung it open and Erin followed her up the path towards her front door.

'It was my pleasure. I had a really lovely time tonight.'

'Except for when I ruined it by bawling my eyes out.'

Erin shook her head. 'You didn't ruin it.'

'You're sure? I felt like there might have been some ugly crying.'

'One beautiful solitary tear trickled down your cheek like it would if you were the heart-broken leading lady in a movie.'

Zoey chuckled and it warmed Erin's heart that she had made her feel better.

'You're sweet to be so kind to me.'

She wasn't sure how to answer that. Shrug it off? Make out it was nothing and it was what friends did?

But she didn't have too much time to ponder on it, for Zoey stepped forward and embraced her in a hug and Erin closed her eyes to absorb every moment of it, her body, her soul, coming alive at the contact. Never wanting it to end. Knowing it would.

And it did.

Zoey stepped back, smiling. 'I'll see you tomorrow.'

Erin nodded. 'Yes. See you.' She began to

back away, turned around and headed down the path, feeling happy and yet also confused and anguished. She'd hated seeing Zoey be upset by Serena over the phone and she'd loved the fact that she—Erin—could put a smile back on Zoey's face.

The rest of the evening, Erin sat in her cottage, knowing that Zoey was right next door. What was she doing right now? Watching television? Unpacking a box or two? Relaxing in a bath?

The image in her head that she had of Zoey in a bath, head back, eyes closed, wet shoulders, a gleaming collarbone freckled with water droplets…stirred something in her. Something that seemed alive and wild, desperate to escape the confines of her body to satisfy itself. Erin couldn't sit still, couldn't focus, and so she grabbed her front door keys and headed on out.

She would walk it off.

Away from Zoey's cottage, not past it.

Because if she did, she wasn't sure if she'd be able to stop herself from knocking on the door, breathless and uncontrolled, and knowing that she would want to kiss Zoey the second she swung that door wide…

# CHAPTER SIX

'IT LOOKS LIKE an allergic reaction.' Zoey was examining the skin of a patient called Lena Young who'd arrived at the practice itchy and uncomfortable. There were reddened blotches all over her torso, legs, arms and face, but most noticeably, her hands looked sore and swollen. It was a systemic reaction. 'Have you been near anything new? Changed your detergent, that kind of thing?'

Lena nodded. 'I've met this guy and I really like him. He invited me back to his last night to stay over and I woke up like this. Am I allergic to him?'

'Allergic to another human being? No, I don't think so, but you may be allergic to something on him, like a deodorant, or a cologne or maybe something that he has in his house. Open wide. I'd just like to check your throat.'

Lena's throat looked clear, thankfully. No swelling to indicate a threat to her breathing.

'He has cats. Long-haired ones. Could it be those?'

Zoey nodded. 'Could be. Have you ever had pets yourself?'

'No. My mum doesn't like cats and my dad's allergic to dogs.'

'It's usually the dander in their coats that causes the reaction. Have you tried taking any antihistamines?'

'No. I wanted you to see the rash first.'

'That isn't necessary. I would have listened to your description of the reaction, if need be, or you could have taken photos to show me. I would always prefer you to take something to make yourself feel better, rather than you suffer just so I can see a condition. Same if you have a fever. I tell patients to take the paracetamol before coming to see me, because then I'll know if the medicine is working. I'm going to write you a prescription for some strong antihistamines. Take these if you're going to be seeing this fine young gentleman again and if they don't work then do get back in touch with me and we can see what we can do next.'

'All right. Thank you, Doctor.'

'No problem. Take care, Lena, and maybe, if you want to, invite him round to yours instead?'

Lena laughed and waved goodbye. As she opened the door to go, Erin appeared and Zoey instantly felt herself sit up straighter and a genuine smile broke across her face.

She'd had such a good time with Erin yesterday, even if Serena had tried to derail her evening. But afterwards, Erin had been so lovely. So kind. The walk back home in the evening? Blissful. Just walking together, side by side, feeling as if she was with an equal, someone who saw her and heard her and who was easy to talk to and listen to. Erin was wonderful. And when she'd hugged her goodbye, she'd had to fight the urge to kiss her on the cheek, knowing that if she did, she might linger and ruin everything, because surely Erin didn't think of her in that way, even if Zoey did have a big girl crush going on.

'Hey! Everything okay?'

Erin nodded and smiled and came into her room with her hands in the pockets of her trousers. She wore a lovely almost sheer white blouse, through which Zoey could see the delicate straps of Erin's camisole. 'I, er...wanted to ask if you were free Saturday night?'

'I have a date with a load of boxes that need unpacking, but I can blow it off, if need be.' She smiled. 'Why?'

'Well, I know you had a difficult evening last night and a friend of a friend has just got in touch to offer me a couple of tickets to see Ever True in concert—'

'*Ever True!*' They were one of her favourite groups! Two boys, two girls, an acapella group that not only sang great covers of pop songs, but who also had their own unique back catalogue with a song in the current top ten. 'Really?'

Erin nodded. 'Private VIP box. Brighton. Saturday night. Fancy it?'

Of course she did! She'd not been to a concert in years. Her last one had been right before she'd married Brad. And to go with Erin? That would be amazing! A night of singing and dancing and having fun? It was what she needed after all of the stress of moving and Serena's call, and the idea of being alone with Erin sent shivers of delicious anticipation down her spine. If she was reading this wrong, then fine, it would just be a great night with a friend, but if it was something else…?

It was exciting, but also pretty terrifying. There was so much at stake if it all went wrong. *Perhaps I ought to say no? Tell her to take someone else?*

But looking at Erin's face, she couldn't.

Zoey wanted to spend that time with her. It was simply irresistible.

'Thank you. That sounds amazing. I'd love to go with you.'

Saturday night couldn't come fast enough for Erin. When she woke up on Saturday morning she was full of anticipation and excitement, imagining the time she would spend with Zoey. What a great time they would have. How lovely it would be to spend more time in her company.

The past week had been full of secret smiles to one another at work. There'd been a team meeting on Thursday morning for all the medical staff, the doctors, the nurses, led by Keiko, their practice manager. Erin had sat opposite Zoey and during the moment when Keiko had asked everyone to close their eyes and just breathe, they'd sneakily glanced at each other, catching each other's gaze like naughty children, and the way Zoey's mouth would slightly curl upwards at the corners had delighted Erin every time.

She spent most of the Saturday examining her wardrobe, wondering what to wear. Something she'd feel comfortable in, for sure, but also something that would adhere to her chosen style of smart casual. She held up dress after dress, skirt after skirt, and eventually settled on a body-hugging little black halter dress that revealed her shoulders and ended mid-thigh, alongside a pair of black heeled suede ankle boots that she knew showed off her legs, one of her best features.

Examining herself in the mirror minutes before going round to Zoey's, she looked herself in the eye and said *I'm just going for a good time. Nothing has to happen.*

She gave herself a spray of perfume, checked her make-up one last time, gave Pixie the cat a goodbye stroke, then locked up and headed next door, her stomach fizzing with excitement.

When Zoey answered the door, Erin had to take in a breath. 'Wow! You look amazing!'

Zoey blushed. 'So do you!'

Zoey was the yin to Erin's yang, in a short white dress that narrowed at the waist and flared out into a skirt. With her ice blonde hair and silver jewellery at her ears, neck and wrist—as well as a cute little ankle bracelet, dripping with what was either zirconias or diamonds—she looked like a beautiful snow princess.

'Ready to go?' Erin knew she would be proud to walk into the arena tonight with Zoey. She was proud to be with her even in normal clothes, work clothes, but tonight? Looking like that? She felt as if all eyes would be on Zoey. How could they not be? She was stunning tonight.

Erin drove. The trip to Brighton would take about an hour if the traffic was good, which it was. Erin put on a playlist of Ever True songs to get them in the mood for the concert and all the way they sang and laughed and enjoyed themselves, until Erin pulled up at the Glass House

Theatre, a brand-new development that had opened in Brighton a couple of years ago.

'Stay there,' Erin said as she got out of the car and walked around to the passenger side of her vehicle and opened Zoey's door, proffering her hand. 'My lady,' she said, smiling.

Zoey laughed and took her hand, sliding from the vehicle demurely, and though she didn't want to let go, she reluctantly did, to close the door and make sure the car was locked. Then together, they made their way to the entrance.

Like Westcombe, seagulls swooped and flew through the air, calling out their protests, as a soft evening breeze caressed Erin's bare skin. She stole a glance at Zoey, couldn't help but notice her neat waist, the way her perfectly curved calf muscles gently narrowed into delicate ankles. The ankle bracelet glittered in the low sun and for a moment, Erin could imagine Zoey's ankles and feet resting on her lap as she stroked her fingers up Zoey's legs. Touching her soft skin, watching as Zoey's breath would hitch in her throat as Erin's fingers drifted higher and higher, reaching the hem of her dress and beyond…

There was a queue coming out of the door for people collecting their tickets, but Erin already had theirs and she showed them to the smartly dressed doorman and he let them pass through.

Inside the Glass House, huge palm trees and glossy dark green plants whose names she didn't know adorned every place she looked as she led Zoey up the stairs to the left that would take them to their private box. And even though they would be sharing the concert experience with hundreds of others, Erin was glad they would have their own private place to be with one another, making it feel as if the concert was just for them.

They showed their tickets to another guy who looked like your typical nightclub bouncer and they were each given a wristband before the doors to their box were opened and they stepped into the main arena.

Because it was such a wonderful evening, the roof had been retracted and the concert was open-air. Both Erin and Zoey gasped as they looked out at the arena, filled with people below. There were vast arc lights that roamed the crowd and the skies and holding music spilled from the speakers. Inside the private box was a small table filled with edible delights and a line of filled champagne flutes. Erin took two and passed one to Zoey. 'To a great night.'

Zoey smiled and clinked her glass with Erin's. 'To a great night.'

The champagne was cold and bubbly and went down a treat.

'We should take a selfie!' Zoey said, reaching for her mobile phone and then leaning in towards Erin, holding her phone out in front of her.

Erin pressed her head to Zoey's. Could smell the apple from her shampoo and the soap from her skin. She smiled broadly, her arm around Zoey's shoulders as Zoey took their picture and then examined it. 'Oh, we look cute!'

They most certainly did. 'You must send it to me.'

'I'll do it now.' They barely heard the swish of the photo as it winged its way through the ether to Erin's phone.

Below them, on the sound stage, they saw technicians come on to adjust the lights and the line of four microphones that stood in the centre waiting for Ever True. The crowd was singing along to the instrumental holding music, swaying their arms in the air, and Erin watched as Zoey took a photo of the crowd, the smile on her face lighting it up with delight. She liked looking at Zoey. It made Erin feel good.

*Am I being an idiot here? Could she possibly feel that way about me?*

Part of her hoped she did. The scared part? Hoped she didn't. Because then it would be easier. They could just be friends, like they were now. But Erin had been alone for nearly two years now and she missed physical contact. Not just sex, but the easy physical contact you had with someone close to you. Being able to hold their hand. To rest your head on their shoulder. Snuggling together watching a movie. Lying in bed, spooning one another, never wanting to move because the other person fit so right against you it was like heaven.

Erin had sworn to never get into another relationship again, but here she was, wondering if she could have one with Zoey. She could picture it so easily. The two of them. It would be marvellous and she would finally be able to feel free and breathe again after being pent-up for so long.

Below, the stage went dark and the holding music quietened and the crowd roared in anticipation.

Zoey and Erin rose from their seats too, watching, waiting for the lights to go back up to reveal the singers of Ever True. She felt her hand brush against Zoey's and she squeezed her hand into a fist to stop herself from threading her fingers into hers.

And then a spotlight lit up one of the singers and the crowd went crazy, cheering and roaring their approval as the vocalist began to sing the first words of her favourite, *Siren Song*, one of their original tracks.

Over the next ninety minutes, the group sang the songs from their latest album, threw in a few of the older songs that were crowd-pleasers and dazzled the arena with choreography, harmonies and a dazzling light show. Erin and Zoey danced together in the box, singing along with them, laughing, cheering, applauding and then, as the concert came to a close, there was an amazing firework display, colours exploding in the air through the open roof, showering the sky with sparks of light in time with one of their most popular songs, and Zoey turned to Erin, a wide smile on her face as she pointed at the sky, but all Erin could do was look at Zoey and think about how beautiful she was in this moment. How beautiful she was in *all* moments. She thought about how Serena had tried to bring her down the other night. How she had tried to manipulate Zoey into feeling guilty and shameful and neglectful, and she could hardly believe that someone who was meant to love her could treat this woman in such a way. She had a kind, warm heart and Erin felt honoured to know her.

Zoey's eyes sparkled as she gazed at Erin and behind her the fireworks continued to light up the sky, but Erin knew that she was the one looking at the most beautiful thing there and in that moment, as she gazed at her, she felt the air change between them. It became charged. Electric. Zoey's gaze dipped to Erin's lips and then back up again and then something incredible happened.

Zoey took a step towards Erin.

Leaned in. Hesitant. Unsure, at first.

But Erin reached up to cradle Zoey's face as she brought the other woman's lips to her own and they kissed.

Everything seemed to stop in that moment. She was aware of the fireworks in the sky, but it felt as if the fireworks were inside her own body as Zoey gave a little moan that Erin felt. The vibration in her tongue, her lips. Eyes closing as she allowed herself to sink into the pleasure that it was to be kissing Zoey.

She felt the same! She'd not misread this!

Her body came alive at the thought and if she could have locked the door to the private box she would have, but she didn't want to leave Zoey's embrace, didn't want this moment to end, because it was so amazing, so surprising, so dizzying. As if she'd drunk more champagne than she really had, even though she knew she'd only had two glasses. Not enough to be drunk, but feeling like if she let go to take in air she would be reeling about, unsteady, weakened by the ecstasy of Zoey kissing her back.

Her lips were so soft. Just like she'd imagined they would be. Her skin so smooth and perfect, and with Zoey's body pressed up against her own, desire flooded her, washing over her like a wave, and she was happy to drown in it and never come up for air.

Did time slow? To Erin, it felt as if it did. As if she was moving in slow motion and she felt everything. Zoey's lips on hers. The taste of her, strawberries and champagne. Each touch. Every fingertip. Her heart was pounding. Trembling in her chest. Could they stay like this forever? Bodies pressing. Heat building.

The concert forgotten.

Zoey had hoped, but not dared to believe, that Erin was attracted to her and she still wasn't sure how the kiss happened. Had she started it? Or Erin? Maybe they both did? All she knew was that she was feeling alive for the first time in a long time.

She'd always known that she was into women, but she'd pushed that part of her down into the shadows when she'd accepted Brad's ring on her finger. Oh, she'd noticed beautiful women, of course she had, but she'd never done anything about it. She was a married woman and she believed in being faithful, even if her marriage to

Brad had not been one of excitement and exhilaration.

They'd had a comfortable life, she and Brad. It had ambled along, both of them committed to their jobs when they'd accepted that children were never going to happen for them. They'd discussed IVF, but Zoey had never pushed for it. The idea of sticking herself with all of those needles, of being poked and prodded for months at a time, had never appealed and, if she was honest with herself, she'd never fully committed to the idea of having kids with Brad. Because she'd never been the real Zoey with him; she had rebounded into a relationship with him and kind of just accepted her fate. Their intimacy together had been infrequent and though it was occasionally satisfying, it had never been full of the fireworks she could feel right now kissing Erin.

*This felt real.*

*This felt right.*

*Genuine.*

As if she'd been a caterpillar for most of her life and now she was suddenly transforming into a butterfly, stretching her wings and basking in the warmth of a sun that she had not felt for nearly two whole decades.

And it was terrifying.

She didn't know how to be this person and,

shocked by how she was feeling, she suddenly let go, took a step back, lips swollen from the intensity of their kissing, and stood there, looking at Erin, fingertips pressed to her disbelieving lips, heart thumping, pulse racing loudly in her ears, wondering just what the hell had she allowed to happen.

They worked together! This was her colleague at a brand-new job, she had moved away from all she knew, uprooted her safe, secure life to come here, and she was risking it all for a fumble at a concert with a woman she considered her only friend.

'Sorry… I, er…don't know what came over me…' she mumbled, gathering her bag, her things, picking up her phone, making sure she had everything, showing that she thought they ought to go. Erin was her ride home. She would have to endure a very uncomfortable drive back to Westcombe now, unless she got herself a taxi. An *expensive* taxi. *Could I call Hazel to come and get me? Probably not.*

'Oh…it's fine.'

But Erin didn't look like it was fine. She looked confused. Shocked even. Discombobulated. She grabbed her own bag that she'd draped over the back of one of the chairs and went to the door and opened it. 'After you.'

Zoey could still feel the pressure of Erin's lips

on her own. How it had felt to feel this woman's tongue slide into her mouth. How her own body had felt. How it had cried out for more. But she had to be logical about this. Think it through. With that kiss they had risked an awful lot and Zoey had come to Westcombe to be happy. To start a new life. She couldn't afford to screw it up this early by kissing a colleague. *A neighbour! She lives right next door to me!*

What would Hazel think? Serena? Geoffrey? She'd never told anyone that she liked women. It hadn't seemed important once she'd married Brad, even if it was a piece of information that had simmered away in the back of her brain her entire life. They seemed accepting of gay people, said it all the time, but would it be different when it came to her? Her in-laws might have something to say about it. Figure she was betraying Brad, or had maybe strayed during the marriage, even though she hadn't. And she didn't want gossip starting in Westcombe either. She had to live there. Work there.

She slipped past Erin, feeling the other woman's eyes on her and her fingers itched for contact as she sidled past the woman who a minute ago had meant *everything*.

They were the first ones leaving and so they were able to exit the Glass House and walk down the steps and find their car and get in and begin driving without being held up. Ever True still pumped from the speakers, reminding her of the concert, and the song coming over the speakers was the exact song the group had been playing as they'd kissed and how she had felt and Zoey felt tears spring to her eyes as she gazed out of the window and fought the urge to cry.

What must Erin think of her? She didn't want to lose her friendship. She sucked in a breath and tried to steady her nerves, get control of her breathing and her voice and said, 'I hope we can pretend that that didn't happen, Erin. Your friendship means a lot to me and I don't want it to be awkward for either of us at work.'

'It won't be.'

But her voice sounded clipped to Zoey. Terse and abrupt.

*Have I ruined everything already?*

She felt so afraid. She'd never stepped out of her lane with Brad and he had been a safe harbour in which she could hide throughout life. He had scooped her up after that disaster with Violet all those years ago and maybe it was that. Maybe she just feared the rejection that had happened after that time with Violet. That somehow, she wasn't enough for another woman. That she'd just been a plaything, someone for Violet to pass the night with, and she feared that happening now. That Erin might use her like a plaything and then discard her.

The rest of their journey, the voices of Ever True filled the car but their own were silent and when they got back to their cottages they both said goodnight in the car and walked to their own individual homes and closed their doors.

## CHAPTER SEVEN

'SO, HOW ARE you settling in?' Hazel asked, looking around at all the boxes that Zoey had not yet unpacked.

'Yeah, fine.' Zoey placed a mug of tea down in front of her sister. Yes, there were still a lot of boxes to unpack, but she was getting there. It took time. She was still sorting through old belongings, deciding what to keep, what to throw, what could go to the charity shops, and she was doing it alone, alongside a full-time job. 'How are you doing? Sickness easing off yet?'

Hazel took a sip of her tea, nodding. 'Finally! Honestly, all those people that swear that morning sickness only lasts for the first three months need to be re-educated.' She rubbed at her swollen abdomen. 'She kicks a lot.'

'That's a good sign.'

Zoey gazed at her sister's growing abdomen and wondered how things might have been between her and Brad if they'd ever had children. Brad had definitely wanted to be a dad. He was the one who'd pushed for it, even though Zoey had been more reluctant. But she'd figured she was married and that was what married couples did and so she came off birth control, figuring that if she did fall pregnant she might feel differently. Only it had never happened. But if there had been a child, or children, she could never have imagined escaping her in-laws, who would have insisted on being able to see their grandchildren.

It had all worked out just fine. She could enjoy children vicariously through her sister. Going to the private scan with her the other week had been wonderful. To see the baby on screen. Her future niece! It was a marvel and she was very much looking forward to being a fun auntie.

'You look tired,' Hazel said.

'I was up late. Couldn't sleep.'

'Oh, yeah, the concert! That was last night. How was it?'

'Ever True were amazing. To hear them harmonise live? It was magical.'

'Why doesn't your face say that? What's wrong?'

'Nothing! It was just a long night. I'm tired,' she lied.

'What time did you get back?'

Zoey shrugged. 'I don't know. Ten thirty? Eleven?'

'You must have been buzzing!'

She smiled and sipped her own tea. How could she tell her sister that the reason she didn't get any sleep wasn't because she was buzzing from the concert but because of the fact that she'd lain there thinking about the kiss with Erin?

How could something that felt so right in the moment make her feel that she'd made a terrible mistake? Risked everything? Work. Their friendship. Zoey had even felt like she didn't want to leave the house in case Erin saw her in the street and asked to talk to her!

Because she didn't know what to say.

She'd never thought that she would get involved with anyone this quickly. She'd imagined being here a good year or two before she started dating and putting herself out there. But she'd concluded that she'd kissed Erin because they'd both just been caught up in the moment, the wonder of the evening. A night of love songs and ballads. The crowd singing along. The lights. The magical display put on by the group. Swaying along with Erin to the music, their arms around one another. It had felt intimate. Zoey had felt so good! So cherished and warm and happy and when Erin had looked at her with longing, Zoey had simply been unable to resist kissing her. To seek out that physical contact that she'd not had for so long. When had she last been intimate with Brad before he'd passed? Months. And then the two years of grieving, adjusting to her new normal, waiting for probate to sort itself out so she could sell the house and make her move for freedom, escaping the clutches of Serena and Geoffrey.

And everyone else seemed to be living their lives whilst she'd felt as if she was on a permanent pause. Even Hazel was changing. Transitioning to her new role as a future mother, having a future to look forward to, even though it was scary for her to become a mother alone. So, just for a moment, she'd looked for something herself and found it in Erin. And it wasn't as if Erin had rejected her. She'd kissed Zoey as much as Zoey had kissed her. It had been mutual attraction. Mutual tenderness and adoration.

'I was buzzing.' *Buzzing from a kiss!* 'It took me a long time to get off to sleep.'

She held the secret of what she'd done within her. Like a pearl in an oyster. She didn't want to spoil it by sharing it with her sister yet, who still did not know that Zoey liked women. She was spoiling the moment enough herself; she didn't need her sister to tell her she'd made a terrible mistake.

'Wish I could have gone with you.'

'That would have been nice. Maybe next time?'

'Next time I'll probably need a babysitter. Do you think Dr Bramley would be up to do that?'

Zoey flushed at the mention of Erin's name and hoped it wasn't too noticeable. 'You'd have to ask her.'

'Maybe I will. Go round there right now and book her in advance.' Hazel chuckled to herself. 'Though she's probably still in bed.'

Erin. In bed.

Zoey didn't want to think about what that would look like too much. Imagining it, imagining Erin in *her* bed, made her own body fizz with excitement and arousal. It was too much! She put down her mug and got up to see if she could find a packet of biscuits in the cupboard.

Anything to not let Hazel see how much their talk of Erin was affecting her.

When she arrived at the practice on Monday morning, Erin glanced into Zoey's room as the door was open and saw her sitting at her desk working.

'Good morning,' she said, determined to be polite and friendly.

'Morning.' Zoey smiled, but it wasn't one of those genuine smiles she usually gave, which brightened her eyes and made Erin's world feel warmer.

'Catching up on admin?'

Zoey nodded. 'You know how it is, if you don't stay on top of it.'

'Mm. I'd better do the same. I'll catch you later.'

'Okay.'

Erin went into her room, shaking her head at how they'd both royally screwed this up. She'd known it was a risk kissing Zoey and yet she'd still done it and now work was going to be awkward and difficult. She slid her bag under her desk and switched on the computer and let out a big sigh. She didn't want it to be this way.

This had echoes of the feelings she'd had with Jenna. The knowledge that they would keep bumping into one another and it becoming so unbearable that one of them left. Erin did not want to have to leave, so she had to make this right.

Not even thinking, she got up and headed back to Zoey's room, walked in and closed the door behind her.

Zoey looked up, her face perturbed and slightly alarmed. 'Erin…?'

'I can't do this.' She still held the door handle behind her back, anchoring herself in the position furthest from this woman she really liked. 'I don't want to have to feel like I'm walking on eggshells here. This is where I work! I love my job! I love the friendship I was building with you.' She paused, thinking her next words over carefully as she let go of the door handle and sat down in the patient's chair next to Zoey's desk. 'What happened at the concert happened. We both got caught up in a moment, that's all. It doesn't have to mean anything. It doesn't have to make us feel like we can't share the same space.' She leaned forward and smiled. 'You're my friend and I'd like you to remain my friend. So we kissed! Big deal! We were celebrating and caught up in that wonderful music. It's the power of that band. They make you think of love and passion and adoration and you and I… we like each other. But let's not ruin what we have here. I need to know that I can spend time with you and not feel like you're trying to escape being with me.'

The kiss had meant a great deal to Erin. It had rocked her world and tipped it on its axis and she still felt all topsy-turvy because of it. But she valued their friendship more.

Zoey let out a long sigh and nodded, smiling. A genuine one this time. The kind that Erin loved. 'You're right. It doesn't have to mean anything. We can go back to being who we were *before* the concert.'

Erin laughed in relief, even if, deep down, she felt a little sad that what had happened could be dismissed so quickly. 'Good. Great! So we're okay, me and you? I can pop in and chat with you? Share our lunchtime together still?'

Zoey laughed too, relief flooding her face. 'Of course!'

Good. Because Erin knew she couldn't risk falling for Zoey. To love again. To expose the raw nerve-endings of her heart. She'd only just begun to heal. She'd only just begun to live again. Falling for Zoey had not been on her bingo card this summer. Being in Westcombe was about her fresh start, not to repeat the mistakes of the past by being with someone who was unavailable. Who would be a terrible mistake. When she did date again, she would do so when she felt absolutely sure she was with the right person. Someone without baggage, someone who would be easy to be with, and Zoey didn't fit any of those criteria. You didn't dip your nib in the company ink and you most certainly did not fall for a colleague and next-door neighbour! It was asking for trouble and she'd had enough trouble to last herself a lifetime.

'Great! Well, I'll let you get to it then and I'll see you at lunch.'

'Yes, you will.'

Erin got up from her chair, having felt a weight be lifted from her chest by confronting the issue head-on. It was the only way to do things sometimes. Maybe if Jenna had done the same thing with her, then they wouldn't have ended up in the mess that they did. Instead, she'd pretended that everything was fine and yet all the while she was seeing an ex, sleeping with him and getting pregnant by him and secretly planning to leave her! They could have just talked. But Jenna and Erin had ignored their problems. Erin had figured that Jenna was acting the way she was because she was getting over the latest IVF disappointment in her own way.

And she did it by betraying Erin and making a mockery of everything she'd thought they were—committed.

Back in her own room, she felt proud of the fact that she'd confronted the issue with Zoey. She'd learned that there was no point in pretending that everything was fine in life. If there was an issue, you should deal with it head-on.

That way, everyone knew where they stood.

When it got to lunchtime, despite the threat of grey, stormy clouds in the distance, Erin asked Zoey if she'd like to go for a walk with her and get some fresh air. That she knew a nice little walk along the headland.

'Sounds great.'

They collected their lunches from the staff room fridge and headed out.

* * *

A narrow path led them up along the headland and to the top of the hill, where there were a few picnic benches and a stone commemorating those from Westcombe who had lost their lives at sea.

The wind up there buffeted them and Zoey had to keep tucking her hair behind her ears. 'I don't like the look of that cloud over there on the horizon. Think we're going to get a storm?'

'Maybe. But hopefully, we can have our lunch before it gets here. I just wanted to show you this spot because it's so beautiful. I come up here to paint the view sometimes. I wish I had my paints with me right now, to capture that sky.'

Zoey looked at her, standing there gazing at the far-off storm clouds, the strong wind whipping at Erin's clothes, pulling at her normally so tamed hair so that it had become this wild mass of honey blonde waves, dancing in the air, obscuring her face.

She'd been so grateful when Erin had come in to clear the air earlier. It had been so awkward first thing, and honestly? If Erin hadn't have cleared the air then Zoey would have, because she'd not been able to stand it. Erin had been her first friend moving here and she really liked her. To lose her because of some silly moment she'd become wrapped up in would have been terrible. Even if she still had the desire to go up to Erin right now, stand behind her, wrap her arms around Erin's waist and cuddle into her back, resting her own head on Erin's shoulders. Just to hold her close. Just to breathe her in. Here. In this isolated place.

That kiss had been all she could think about and the fact that she desired *more* was terrifying. And they were alone up here. No one to see.

And yet…she was afraid of her own feelings.

Erin turned to face her, hair whipping behind her head now, face unobscured, smiling. 'Let's eat. I'm starving.'

Zoey was most definitely hungry. And not just for food. Her stomach rumbled to let her know it needed sustenance, but it was her body that craved Erin more.

But they'd said they'd just be friends.

Neither of them wanted to ruin the friendship they had begun by risking it for something more, something untested, that could crash and burn, leaving them both stranded alone once again. Better to be alone with a good friend than with no one at all.

'Can I ask you something?' Zoey said as they sat at a picnic bench and began to eat.

'Of course. Anything.'

'Who were you before you came to Westcombe? I mean, you know who I was—who I was with—but I've realised I don't really know anything about you.' Perhaps if she understood Erin more, it would help? Perhaps Erin would tell her that she was a woman who had never had a long-term relationship. Or that she only ever allowed one-night stands, that kind of thing. Because if she did, that would make it easier to tell herself to stay away.

'I was in a long-term relationship with someone who I'd known since we were kids.'

*Damn.*

'Oh! Do you mind me asking what happened?'

Erin shook her head. 'Of course not. You've been open with me. I was with a woman. Jenna. And I loved her ever since I laid eyes on her.'

'And there's never been anyone else?'

'Not for me,' Erin said in a tone that suggested there had been for Jenna.

It was exhilarating to have it confirmed that Erin liked women. That the kiss they'd experienced hadn't been experimental for her.

'We were trying to have a family. Jenna wanted to experience pregnancy and so she agreed that she would be the one to carry the baby, if we were successful.'

'You didn't want to?'

'I wanted kids, but… I never wanted to be the one to do that.' Erin sighed. 'We tried IVF for about five years. We'd been together a long time, we were settled, we were strong and we both felt that the struggle of IVF treatments wouldn't break us.'

'It must have been difficult.'

'It was. But I'd never been so proud of Jenna as I was back then. What she went through. What she endured, changing her body's cycle, the endless injections, the hormone treatments, the discomfort—all so we could have a child…' Erin shook her head, still in awe.

'What happened?' Zoey sensed that this story did not have a happy ending. Erin was here alone in Westcombe and there was no child living in her house.

'The cycles failed. The devastation each time, to realise that all that struggle had been for nothing, was awful. Draining. The experience of IVF is a terrifying rollercoaster. Hoping beyond hope. Imagining life if the test is positive. Thinking of how you'd decorate a nursery. What names you would choose. Planning for a future. They implant an embryo. You know that for a couple of days, at least, you're carrying a baby. Your fingers crossed all the time. Dreaming. Making bargains with God. Praying that it'll work, and then this crashing loss. Grieving for the baby that never took. Having to watch Jenna crumble and blame herself. Comforting one another and trying to find the strength to do it all over again as a promising life literally bleeds out of her time after time.'

Zoey felt guilty. Erin had wanted a child. So had Brad. His parents had been desperate for a grandchild. She'd not really wanted a child with him. It hadn't felt right and she knew it. And she'd been glad it hadn't happened. She had been in a privileged position, to be honest. She'd not had to go through the torment that Erin was describing.

She felt one or two spots of rain and noticed the clouds had come much closer. But Erin had her back to them and was lost in her memories and hadn't noticed. And Zoey didn't want to interrupt her. This was important. Hearing what she'd gone through. It would help her understand where Erin was coming from. It sounded like she'd had a really tough time.

'One time, we implanted, waited a couple of weeks and then got a positive result.' Her face lit up at the memory. 'You can only imagine how we both felt. The weight that lifted off our shoulders, believing that everything was going to be okay, but then, at six weeks, she miscarried.'

'Oh, Erin! I'm so sorry.' She wanted to reach out and place her hand on hers, but fear stopped her. She couldn't. Not after what had happened this morning. How it had been between them. The awkwardness at work—they'd just got past that. And even though friends did comfort one another, it felt too soon to be reaching out and touching her.

'Jenna got very depressed then. She withdrew. When she did talk to me, it was to shout and rage at me and then, after a few months, she seemed to brighten. I thought we were getting past it. I thought, maybe it's time to suggest another round? Another try? And when I did, she sat me down and told me there was no need. That she was pregnant, but she'd got pregnant through having an affair with an old boyfriend. And that she was leaving me to start a life with him.'

Zoey stared at Erin. That was awful! To be betrayed in such a manner was inexcusable. She didn't think. She just reached out, laid her hand on Erin's, stroking the back of her hand with her thumb. Wishing she could hold her. Wishing she could comfort her. But she never got the chance.

Above, the sky rumbled with sudden thunder and the rain that had been threatening began to lash down.

Neither of them had coats or umbrellas and they were up on the hill, exposed to the elements. 'We'd better make a run for it,' Zoey suggested.

Erin nodded, but they didn't let go of the other's hand as they began to run down the path that would lead them back to Westcombe. At first the rain felt miserable to be in, but then, as they got more and more sodden, they began to laugh with abandon as they made it down into the town and took shelter beneath a shop awning to shake off their clothes and take a breather. Finally, they let go of the other's hand, as if realising what they were doing.

Zoey looked at Erin, bedraggled and sodden, and thought *She still is the most beautiful person I have ever met.* And after her intense revelation, she wanted Erin to know more about her feelings. She had to raise her voice to be heard over the heavy rain.

'I knew someone…before Brad. A girl. Violet. We met at university.'

Erin pulled her hair free from her face and looked at her curiously. 'You did?'

Zoey nodded. 'She was beautiful. Just like you.' She blushed. 'Only *her* hair was pink and she really seemed to like me as much as I liked her. We went out. I spent the night with her and it was the most amazing night of my life. I thought we had something special, but the next day she ghosted me. I thought we had promise, a real connection of hearts and minds and bodies, but she just wanted another notch on her bedpost. Brad scooped me up. Put me back together again and stopped any gossip before it started. When he offered me a future, I felt safe again, but what

I was really doing was putting myself in a self-imposed prison. Never to feel that way again. Excited. Thrilled. I've always hidden my attraction to women.'

A soft hopeful smile appeared on Erin's face. 'And now?'

Zoey smiled. 'I don't know just yet. But I think it could be a real possibility when I'm ready.' She looked out at the sky. The grey clouds were beginning to move on, swept away by the strong breeze, and blue skies were going to come back, even though the fat raindrops still fell in protest. She didn't notice the hopeful look on Erin's face at her words. 'We should make another run for it back to the surgery or we're going to miss afternoon clinic.'

Erin nodded. 'Ready on the count of three?'

Zoey laughed and psyched herself up for another mad dash through the rain.

# CHAPTER EIGHT

'MY ANKLES ARE HUGE!' Hazel moaned as she lifted them up onto Zoey's lap for inspection.

Zoey smiled and began to rub her sister's feet for her. 'They're not. You just feel cumbersome, that's all. These are perfectly normal ankles for a woman in her third trimester.'

Hazel grimaced as she pushed down on her bump. 'Ugh, foot under the rib. Move, won't you?'

'You know you're going to miss all of this when the little one is here?'

'At least I'll have my body back to myself.'

'Will you? You said you were going to breast-feed on demand.'

Hazel seemed to think about that as she sighed at Zoey's expert ministrations, massaging her feet and toes. 'But don't they sleep for like three or four hours in between feeds?'

'If you're lucky. I see some mothers that come to see me because their little one just wants the comfort of being held by their mum, or constantly suckles every twenty minutes or so.'

She opened her eyes and looked at her sister in shock. '*Every twenty minutes?*'

Zoey laughed at her. 'It can happen.'

'But how will I get anything done? How am I going to do this full stop? With no one to help me.'

'I'll help.'

'You have a full-time job.'

'I can still help. At weekends. You could pop round whenever if you need to get out of the house, or I could come to you.'

'Am I a fool thinking I can do this by myself, Zo?'

'Of course not! Plenty of women raise children alone and do so successfully. There's no reason why you can't.'

Hazel sighed. 'I hope so. The closer it gets, the more scared I become.'

'That's normal, too. Now, lie back and try to relax.'

Erin checked and rechecked her living room. It looked perfect. She'd cleaned, tidied, straightened the bookcases and dusted the lamps. Then she'd lit candles around the room, even though it was still daylight outside until after nine in the evening, simply because she liked to see candles flickering and they were scented ones, giving off the warm aroma of black cherries. She'd even put a blanket over the back of the couch, but it was so warm still, even though the recent storm had freshened things up, that she didn't think they'd use it.

She'd asked Zoey if she wanted to pop round for a movie night. One of the channels on her streaming service was having a movie marathon of the top three most romantic movies ever made and the occasion had simply demanded a movie night and bowls of popcorn and maybe even a wine or two. And she'd not wanted to watch them alone and though she loved Pixie, her cat, the feline didn't count as company if she was going to sit and blub into a tissue. She wanted to do that with someone else. Someone she felt comfortable with.

A knock at her door made her jump and her heart pound and she laughed at herself for being so nervous. But she couldn't help it. Hearing Zoey say the other day that she would contemplate a relationship with a woman in the future made the world full of possibilities. And though she'd been married to a guy for fifteen years, she wouldn't be experimenting, because she'd been with a woman before. And even though the logic in her brain screamed at her to not develop feelings for someone who also liked men, because of what had happened with Jenna, she simply couldn't stop her moments of fantasy in which she dreamed of her and Zoey together.

One last check in front of the mirror. Her sleeveless white crop top with a pink denim miniskirt made her look good and she knew it. And she padded barefoot to the front door and swung it open wide with a smile.

Zoey stood there, holding a small bunch of fresh flowers and a bottle of Prosecco. Adorable in a red sleeveless minidress. 'These are for you,' she said, thrusting them forward.

'Thank you! Come on in.' She accepted the gifts and stepped back, inhaling Zoey's flowery perfume as she passed her by. This was the first time Zoey had been in her cottage. 'I'll put these in water then I'll give you a tour.'

The flowers were pretty. Pink carnations, gerberas and white roses, encircled by wood-fern greenery. 'These are beautiful,' she said, rearranging them into a vase and filling it with water.

'White roses signal new beginnings, which I thought might be apt.'

Erin smiled at her. 'It's perfect. Do the others have meanings?'

'I'm not sure. Let me look those up.' She pulled out her phone to use the internet. 'It says pink gerberas mean admiration and pink carnations mean gratitude.' Zoey looked up and blushed. 'I didn't know it when I picked them, but I think those fit.'

'Me too. Come on, let me show you around. My cottage is laid out differently to yours.'

She gave Zoey the full tour of the place. Her kitchen and dining area was bigger because the previous owners had knocked a wall through and used the utility room space. Upstairs, she felt herself grow nervous as she showed Zoey her bedroom. It felt an intimate thing to do and she tried to gloss over it and move on, but Zoey spotted Pixie the cat curled up on Erin's bed.

'That's Pixie?'

'Mm-hmm.'

'Can I pet her?'

'Of course!'

They both stepped into the room and Zoey knelt by Erin's double bed and reached out to stroke the cat. Pixie was a tuxedo cat. Black mostly, with white front paws and chest, like a little feline butler. The only other splash of white she had was on the tip of her tail, currently obscured.

Pixie purred and leaned into Zoey's cuddles.

'She likes you.'

Zoey laughed. 'Aww! I love her. I wonder if I should get a cat? Brad never wanted animals. Said he was allergic.'

To Erin it was another reminder of how Zoey had made herself a lot smaller to fit into Brad's world. That she'd shut down parts of herself and made herself numb. At what cost?

'There's a cat rescue in the next town.'

Zoey stood. 'I should finish unpacking probably before I get a cat. I'd probably lose it to the boxes and accidentally throw it out, or something.'

'Probably.' She liked standing there watching Zoey in her bedroom, crouched by her bed, her head laid on the bedspread as she smiled at Pixie. What would it be like to wake up in the morning and see Zoey's head on the pillow across from her? The thought made Erin go all hot. 'Shall I get us some drinks? What would you like? Shall I open the Prosecco?'

Zoey stood and smiled at her. 'Sounds perfect.'

Erin led the way back downstairs and into the kitchen. 'First movie starts at seven. So we've got a few minutes before it starts. Popcorn?'

'Lovely! Can I help with anything?'

'No. You go take a seat in the living room and I'll bring through the drinks and snacks.'

Had this been a bad idea to invite Zoey around? What it was doing to her emotionally… as if she was on a knife-edge, not knowing how she should feel. The kiss haunted her still. How

Zoey had made her feel. Seen. Adored. Attractive. *Wanted.* Then running through the rain with her holding her hand. That moment under the shelter when Zoey had confessed she'd been with a woman before. The hope was killing her inside, because they'd sworn to be friends only, but…

Was it wrong to hope for more? To imagine it? To dream it?

It was just so difficult when you felt like possible happiness was so close! But if they got it wrong, if it didn't work out, if Zoey met a guy she liked more than Erin, then…her heart would be broken again and she didn't want to have to be heartbroken over Zoey. And imagining her with someone else was…

Well, she didn't want to think about that.

She brought through two glasses of Prosecco and a tray with popcorn, cookies and some strawberries she'd washed and hulled, settling herself onto the couch next to Zoey. The credits for the first movie were just beginning and they settled in to watch the movie.

They *awwed* and *oohed.* Gasped when it looked like the heroine was being betrayed, then had all the feels and, in Zoey's case, a tear in the eye when they finally got their happy ending. The second movie was more contemporary, a young woman desperately in need of work found a job looking after a quadriplegic man and they fell in love. But the ending was sad and had them both bawling and sniffing into tissues. But the final movie of the three was more upbeat, comedic, sassy. A working girl hired to stay for a week with a rich guy in his penthouse. At the end, when the hero climbed the fire escape despite his fear of heights and rescued his fair maiden, they both felt emotionally wrung-out.

Darkness had fallen and somehow, during the evening, they had both ended up beneath the same blanket on the couch, Zoey leaning against Erin as the final credits rolled. The Prosecco was gone. The popcorn bowls were empty and only crumbs remained where cookies had previously sat.

'That was amazing,' Zoey said, yawning and stretching like a cat.

'It was.' Erin didn't dare move, fearing that if she did, Zoey would move away from her, and she liked the way they were snuggling right now. Was this how it would be if they ever got together?

She laid her head against Zoey's, closing her eyes and imagining that this was somehow different. That the two of them were a couple. That they'd moved beyond the awkward dating phase and were in the in love and nothing could tear them apart phase. It felt peaceful. Calm. The desire to turn ever so slightly and lay a kiss atop Zoey's head was strong and she fought it. Not wanting to scare Zoey off again.

What was she thinking right now, as the credits continued to roll? Would she get up? Say it was time she went home? Or did she feel like Erin did? Not wanting to move? Wanting to stay where they were forever?

'It's late,' Zoey said.

*Ah. Here we go.*

'Of course.'

'I'm going over to Hazel's first thing tomorrow. Better not have a late night.'

'Okay.'

But still, she didn't move.

Could Zoey hear how loudly Erin's heart was thumping?

And then something strange, something crazy, happened. Afterwards, Erin would still be unable to work out what had happened, but she thought that they both moved at the same time. Both went to stand up, both grabbed at the blanket to fold it up and somehow ended up standing, facing one another, really close, just the blanket between them.

Standing there in the dark, their faces lit only by the last dying flickers of the candles, they stared at one another. It was like being back at the concert. Together, in the dark. Close. Intimate.

Erin noticed a single stray strand of Zoey's white blonde hair caught in her mouth and she reached up slowly, hesitantly, to remove it.

Zoey's lips parted, her breathing became quite heavy.

She looked so beautiful! It was an agony to not be able to touch her. Every nerve-ending felt as if it would self-combust, her skin tingling and feeling as if it was as hot as the surface of the sun. But Erin would not make a move unless she did.

'Thank you…for tonight. I had a great time,' Zoey said in a low, breathy voice.

Was she struggling with this just as much as Erin?

'Me too.'

'I…' Zoey was searching Erin's face, staring deeply into Erin's eyes, and then, wondrously, Zoey pressed her lips against hers!

Erin closed her eyes in bliss, paralysed by fear, nervous of reacting too strongly, not wanting to scare Zoey off, but she also didn't want Zoey to think that she didn't want this!

A low moan escaped her as the kiss deepened and she could not help but cradle her face and feel Zoey's body pressed against hers as her world exploded and every sane thought left her brain until nothing was left except how Zoey was making her feel.

But then Zoey suddenly stepped away and

looked at her in fear. In doubt. Worry. 'What are we *doing*? *Again?*'

'It's okay. We can take this as slowly as you need.'

Zoey pressed her fingertips to her lips. 'What if it all goes wrong?'

'Who says it will go wrong?'

'Have you ever been in a relationship in which it hasn't?'

Erin had no answer she wanted to say out loud.

'I don't know what to do, Erin. I can't stop thinking about you and that terrifies me.'

'It terrifies me, too. But, like I say, we can do this at a glacial pace, if you need. There's no pressure here from me. I can wait until you're ready. I need to go slowly, too.'

It hurt to say it, because Erin didn't want to wait at all! But there was no other choice. This wasn't simple. They were neighbours, they worked together. They lived in a small community where gossip could run rife and spoil reputations in an instant, and she did not want them to be known as the two doctors at the surgery who had fallen for one another and then fallen apart. And once upon a time, she'd believed that she and Jenna would be forever and look at how that had turned out. Betrayal. Abandonment. As if her life, her love had meant nothing. That she'd not been enough for Jenna. Who knew if she'd be enough for Zoey?

So…if that meant taking it slow and going at a snail's pace, then she would.

Because Zoey was worth waiting for.

And her own heart needed all the protection in the world that she could give it.

# CHAPTER NINE

KATE WALLANDER, A WOMAN who'd just turned forty years of age, came into Zoey's consultation room and sat down. She looked anxious.

Zoey had scanned her medical history. Nothing much of note, no ongoing conditions. One or two occasions in which her iron levels had been low and a bout of Covid in 2020 that had put her in hospital, but nothing except a smear test since then.

'Morning! How can I help?'

Kate smiled nervously. 'I've, er…got a bit of a problem down below.'

'Okay. Can you tell me more about it?'

Kate's cheeks had gone red. 'I first noticed a couple of weeks ago. A bit of, well, discomfort? I thought it might be my age, approaching perimenopause or something—my mum had hers early too—but, I don't know. Something just doesn't feel right and there's more discharge.'

'All right. Can you describe this discharge?

Has the colour changed? Is it the viscosity or simply the amount?'

'I'm not sure. It's just not the stuff I'm used to. Maybe it's a different colour? I'm not sure.'

'That's okay. Any bleeding? Pain?'

'A little.'

Zoey nodded, thinking. 'And have you had any new partners or unprotected sex lately?'

She blushed again. 'My husband and I separated a couple of years ago. I swore I'd never date again, but you know how it is. You get lonely. You drink too much wine and your best friend suggests you go on a dating app and before I knew it, I'd put up a profile and starting dating again.' She paused. 'I've slept with three new guys over the last year. We used protection each time, but the last one… I'm still dating him and a couple of weeks ago, we got a bit carried away in the moment and…'

'And you didn't use a condom?'

Kate winced and nodded, cheeks redder than ever. 'You don't have to tell me off any more than I've been doing myself.'

Zoey felt for her. What a nightmare to be in! 'Are you still seeing him?'

'We were both so lonely. It just seemed a simple thing for us both to just scratch an itch without commitment, you know?'

'Is he sleeping with other partners?'

'He says not.'

'Does he have any symptoms?'

'I've not asked him. I've been trying to avoid his calls to be honest, until I got this sorted.'

'And you've no history of having a sexually transmitted infection before?'

'No! Me and my husband were both virgins before we got married. We wanted our wedding night to be special and we stayed true to one another our entire married lives. We wanted to have a baby, but it never happened for us.'

Zoey heard the longing in the woman's voice. Kate had wanted her husband's baby. Erin had wanted a baby with her ex. Was it wrong that she hadn't?

'You mention you've had some pain. Let's get you up on the bed and I'll examine your tummy, if that's all right?'

Kate nodded and clambered onto the bed and lifted her top and unbuttoned her jeans.

Zoey palpated her abdomen carefully, but could feel nothing untoward. She helped Kate back up into a sitting position. 'When was your last period?'

'A month ago. I'm a little late.'

'Okay. I'm going to give you a swab and a urine bottle. Go into the bathrooms here and use the swab first.' She gave instructions on how to do so. 'Then I want you to give me a urine sample. We'll do a quick pregnancy test and see what the swab comes back with.'

'Okay.'

When Kate had left, Zoey tapped in the notes so far onto her patient's record. The world of dating was so complicated right now. Maybe it always had been? But you had to be so careful these days. She thought of Erin. Had she worried about catching something when she'd realised her partner had been sleeping with a guy? It was never anything Zoey had had to worry about and nor did she want to. There were so many things you had to worry about and STIs were so prevalent.

When Kate returned, Zoey checked the swab against the results, looking for chlamydia and gonorrhea. She also dipped the urine. When she had both results, she sat back down at her desk. 'Okay, so this is positive for chlamydia, I'm afraid.'

Kate nodded, taking it in. 'Oh.'

'And the pregnancy test is negative. You might be a little late because of the infection, but it's very straightforward to treat. I'm going to prescribe you some doxycycline to take for a week and I'd advise you to not have sex for at least seven days. Your partner will also have to have treatment, so I advise that he go and see his GP or go to a genitourinary clinic.'

'Oh God, I'm going to have to tell him!' She looked tense.

'I want you to come back though if you develop a fever or the pain gets worse, or you have bleeding that is beyond your period, as we don't want any complications. This is very common and nothing to be embarrassed about. But you do need to talk to him, especially if he's sleeping with anyone else.'

Kate nodded. 'I can't believe this is happening to me. A sexually transmitted disease! At my age!'

'Age is no barrier to STIs, I'm afraid. It favours no one.'

'Maybe I should stop with this dating nonsense. It's only got me into trouble and more heartache. I mean, what's the point?'

It was a question that Zoey didn't want to think too hard about.

All relationships had costs. You just had to decide whether you were strong enough to pay them.

Erin's next patient was an older gentleman. She'd seen him once before, right at the beginning of her time here in Westcombe, when he'd come in after his marriage split. To say that he was the one who had come in was erroneous. It was more like his daughter had brought him in, concerned that he wasn't eating or sleeping very well. But she'd not seen him since and when he walked into her consulting room on that last appointment of the day, she could see that he had lost quite a bit of weight.

'Hello, Greg. How can I help you today?' He had a sickly pallor, with dark circles under his eyes, and he had aged in the months since she'd seen him last. Skin draped over bone.

'I guess I'm not doing so good. Kitty, my daughter, she said I had to come in.'

'Tell me what's been happening.'

He shrugged. 'Nothing much. Just existing day to day. I'm just finding it hard to find any enjoyment out of life.'

'Are you sleeping?'

'In fits and starts. Better than I was.'

'Eating and drinking?'

Another shrug. 'Not very well. It just seems a lot of energy to cook a meal for one person and my wife always did that. I can make beans on toast, but that's about the size of my cooking repertoire.'

'Would you say you're still feeling quite numb emotionally?'

He nodded this time. 'She was my life. I gave my wife everything I had. My heart. My soul. My love. And it wasn't enough for her. Said I didn't fulfil her. Didn't give her what she needed…and it's just left me feeling like…what's left? If all of me, all of my attention, all of my dedication, all of my love wasn't enough, then what is the point? I'll never be enough. It's made me feel like I have nothing to offer anyone and though Kitty comes round and she brings the kids and they seem happy enough with me, I still feel like the point of me just isn't there. It's made me have a few dark thoughts. Intrusive thoughts.'

Erin nodded. She knew those feelings. Had felt them herself once upon a time. 'Do you have any thoughts about harming yourself?'

And even though he'd alluded to that in his previous response, he seemed unwilling to accept that that was what he'd been doing. 'Maybe? I don't know. They're fleeting. Never around long enough for me to give them any serious thought, but…they're there. I'm aware they're there. Lurking. I don't want—and Kitty doesn't want—those thoughts to get any worse.'

'Would you act on them, do you think?'

He shook his head. 'No. I don't think so.'

There was still uncertainty though and Erin had a duty to safeguard her patient. 'Have you talked to anyone about this? Had any therapy?'

'No. I've never been that sort of person.'

'I think it might help you to talk to someone about how you're feeling. Someone who can help you move through this process. You're grieving the end of your marriage and it very much sounds to me like it wasn't your choice. This is something that happened to you. You never fell out of love with your wife and she's left you.'

Erin knew the pain of this. She'd still loved Jenna very much. Still thought that they were both working on their relationship. Finding small moments of happiness in between the drama of the IVF treatments. Finding ways of showing Jenna that she loved her. Would support her. Be there for her. But it hadn't been enough for Jenna. The one thing she'd wanted—a baby—Erin couldn't give her. The doctors couldn't give her. The IVF kept failing. And so she'd found someone who could. An ex-boyfriend, of all people! Someone she'd already left for a damned good reason. But, by all accounts, Jenna and he were still together. Raising their little family. And Erin had been left, like Greg, to somehow carry on, to slowly allow that love to die. A love that had once burned so brightly had had to become an ember that she could stamp out.

'These things take time to get over,' she said, talking from experience. 'And it really does help to speak to someone impartial. I'm going to refer you to talking therapy, so you can speak to someone who can give you some coping mechanisms to get through this chapter in your life.

You very much sound depressed and I'm wondering if you'd also consider an antidepressant?'

Her own doctor had prescribed them for her. She'd been reluctant at first. Doctors always made the worst patients. But eventually she'd given in and they had helped.

'You offered me those before.'

'I did. They can take a few weeks to get into your system and have any effect, but in your case, the fact that you're suffering still, have no enjoyment from life, aren't eating properly… I think these, alongside therapy, will help you.'

He nodded. 'All right. I'll give them a try. Kitty said I should take them if they're offered.'

'Good. I'm going to book you in for a telephone appointment in two weeks' time and then another a month after that, see how you're doing. But if those thoughts get worse in the meantime, you're to call the surgery immediately, understood?'

'Yes. I will.'

Feeling reassured, she said goodbye and watched him go. She felt hopeful for him. He had a daughter. Family. Someone to look out for him and care for him. Erin had not. She'd lost her parents early in life and as an only child, she was used to keeping all her worries and concerns to herself. When it had all fallen apart with Jenna, she had been able to up sticks and go to Westcombe. Uprooting her life and just going at a moment's notice. Even if she did feel like she'd left one small part of her heart behind with Jenna. She'd believed that she would never heal. That there would always be a scar on her heart and that she would have nothing to give to another person.

Until Zoey showed up.

And now, she was beginning to believe that maybe she could be capable of loving again. Her attraction, her desire, her emotions for Zoey were sometimes all that she could think about.

Would Zoey hurt her the way Jenna had—if she allowed herself to continue what she and Zoey had begun? They'd agreed to take it slow and that was a good thing. That way, both of them could back out at any moment. Not risk their damaged hearts, even if that would devastate Erin if she did that.

But she didn't want to turn out to be a Greg. She didn't want to be grieving for what she'd lost all the time. Life was about living. About experiencing all that it had to offer. Perhaps there was a reason why Zoey was in her life right now and she could use it to change and grow, rather than remain stagnating the way she had been.

Zoey was her bright light in the darkness and she could do nothing but go towards it.

# CHAPTER TEN

'YOU EVER SEE that film where the monster bursts out of the body?' Hazel asked, squirming in her seat.

Zoey smiled. 'Yes.'

'That's what this pregnancy feels like. Honestly, I got no sleep last night. Baby kept stretching and rolling and kicking. At one point, I thought she was trying to kick her way out. Gave me horrible indigestion.'

'One day, you'll look back on this time fondly and reminisce.'

'Not sure I'll have the time.'

'Why not?'

'Hello? I'm gonna be a single parent here! Do you know how hard that is?'

'Not personally, no.'

Hazel saw her face and looked guilty. 'Sorry. I know you and Brad tried.'

Zoey flushed. Not as hard as Hazel thought. 'It's fine. It was meant to be.'

'You'd have made a great mum. In fact, there's

still time! You could still meet someone and have a baby!'

Zoey shook her head. 'I don't think so.' She wasn't looking for another relationship with a guy. That had been the wrong choice for her. And she'd stayed with it for far too long because she'd grown comfortable and, honestly, Brad had never made that many demands on her. Not sexually. Not emotionally. They'd been roommates more than anything else and they'd bumbled along through life, going through the motions because it had been easier than asking for what they really wanted. Zoey had always been afraid to ask for what she wanted out of life. Had always been a follower, rather than a leader. And if she got together with Erin properly one day?

The idea, the *possibility* of it, thrilled her.

And terrified her at the same time.

*Why have I never told Hazel about my true sexuality?*

'You've got ages before you hit menopause. There's still a chance.'

'To be as miserable as you?' Zoey asked with a wink to lighten the seriousness of the conversation.

'Misery loves company,' Hazel replied, wincing and pressing down on her belly, where a foot was no doubt caught up under her ribs.

'You're not miserable. Are you?'

'No. Just terrified.'

'Of the birth?'

'Oh, completely! But also what comes after.' Hazel bit her bottom lip and worried at it.

'Being a mother?'

Hazel nodded. 'I don't earn much. I live in a small flat above a shop. My baby doesn't have an interested father. Mum and Dad live in another bloody country! You work full-time… What if I need help? What if I struggle? What if… I can't do it on my own?'

Zoey could hear the plaintive distress in her sister's voice. This was a real concern for her. And though she often joked and minimalized her distress, this worry was clear to see.

She'd always helped out her sister whenever she could. Hazel had lived with her and Brad for a few years when their parents had emigrated. It had been so good for them to rediscover their bond back then and when Hazel had left, leaving Zoey and Brad alone, she'd realised just how alone she'd been feeling. Being able to reconnect with her sister again, as she entered a new phase in her life, meant an awful lot and she did not want to let her sister down. The impending birth had been her sole reason for getting a post in Westcombe. So she could be there for her sister and she would not let her down!

'You won't be alone. I'll be here to help you.'

'Not all the time. You've got your own life. Your work. What if things get hard and I can't reach you because you have a full day's clinic?'

'Hazel, I may have work, but I will *always* be there for you. Even if it means you bringing the baby to the surgery and hanging out in our staff room. I will not let you go through this alone.'

'You mean it?'

Zoey got up and gave her a sister a hug. 'Every word. I will not let you down.'

Hazel squeezed her back. 'Thank you. I love you. You know that, right?'

'I love you, too.'

And though she loved Hazel and the baby that was coming, she still felt a little bit that she was falling into old, comfortable habits. Habits that wouldn't rock the boat. She'd come to Westcombe to be with her sister, but she also wanted and needed her own life.

Would it become subsumed by looking after Hazel and the baby?

Would she ever have any freedom at all?

And perhaps freedom was just as illusion? Something people chased, but never really got to have?

'Have you got everything?' Erin asked.

Zoey looked down at the assembled bags at

her feet. 'Food—check! Drinks—check! Painting supplies—check!'

Erin smiled. 'Great. Let's load the car up and then we'll go. It's a fabulous day for it and I know the perfect spot that gives us a view of the cove and Westcombe Bay.' She reached down to help Zoey pick up her bags right at the moment that Zoey did the same. Their hands went for the same bag and her touch was electric. They both stood back up, blushing. 'Sorry. You, er…you take that one and I'll take the others?'

Zoey was pink-cheeked too and gratefully she nodded her agreement.

It was silly getting embarrassed over that, but she and Zoey had agreed not to rush things and she did not want Zoey to think or feel that she was pushing for more when Zoey might not be ready yet. Taking it slow was going to be agonising, but it was also going to be sensible. For both of them. They'd both been burned in the past and neither of them wanted to rush madly into anything that was going to be a terrible mistake, especially when there was so much at stake for them.

But going slow didn't mean avoiding taking the time to develop their connection and so Erin had popped into Zoey's consulting room during the week and suggested that at the weekend they go up onto the bluffs and paint together—

something they both loved doing. Suggesting a date that had zero pressure and zero expectations seemed a good idea. Whereas at the same time, they could both indulge in a pleasure they both enjoyed—watercolour painting.

Erin drove them through Westcombe and up and out on the cliff road to the west of the small town. It took them up a winding route, through verdant tree tunnels and alongside fields, until they reached a small turnoff down a small lane that Erin took, knowing that it would bring them out in a small parking area where there was a viewing spot of the town, the harbour and the sweep of beach far below. And the best thing? There was hardly any wind today, so they'd be able to set up their easels and not worry about things flying away, or having to weigh down papers with stones.

After parking, Erin opened up the boot of the car and lifted out their bags and then together they walked over to the viewing spot. There was no one else there yet and they had the place to themselves.

'Wow! Amazing!' Zoey said as she looked down at the bay, the glittering water and the tiny people like ants far below, occupying the beach. 'You were right about the view.'

'Beautiful, isn't it?'

Zoey turned to smile at her, hand up to shield her eyes from the sun. 'It is.'

'Let's get set up.'

Together, they brought all their things from the car and set up two easels, close enough together so that they could talk easily to one another, but not so close that they could see each other's painting. They'd already agreed in the car that they wanted to see each other's work as a surprise at the end.

The sun was beating down overhead, but luckily, Erin had a solution—clamps that would hold a parasol over each of their heads to provide a bit of shade, and once they'd got set up with all their art equipment and a glass of non-alcoholic wine each, they set to work.

'I saw Hazel a few days ago,' Zoey said.

'How is she doing? She must be getting close to delivering soon.'

'She is. Another month to go. I think she's half wishing it would never end, but also glad for it all to be over. Apparently carrying during the summer months is not ideal.'

'It can be a problem.'

'She's scared of being a mum, but I think everyone is at some point, especially when it's your first.'

'She strikes me as a very capable young woman.

Does she have a partner? I know she was single the last time I saw her.'

'No one that I know of.'

They were getting their first daubs of paint on the canvases. Erin was going for a landscape picture. She wanted to capture the vastness of the sea, the nature of its fluidity and movement contrasted against the stillness of the sky.

She had no idea of what Zoey was painting. What aspect of the view she was focusing on. But she stole glances at her on occasion. There was a grace to Zoey and her movements. The way she held her brush. The delicate way she dipped it in the water and then patiently pressed the brush against the jar to rid it of the excess. The considered way she thought for a moment, before pressing brush to canvas. She really was beautiful. Graceful. Standing there like some nymph in a white vest top and a short denim dungaree dress that ended at mid-thigh. Face shadowed by the parasol above her. Biting at her lower lip as she thought and pondered and considered.

Erin could feel her heart pounding just looking at her and had to look away to gather her own breath, slow down her pulse rate and concentrate on her own painting. It was coming on nicely. She was happy with what she had. And knew she could make it better, but wasn't sure how.

'There's something missing. Would you take a look at what I've done so far and tell me what you think?' This was a first for Erin. Painting was what she did just for herself. She'd never really shown her work to anybody or tried to sell it and letting Zoey look at it, now, unfinished, felt scary. But she also knew that she valued Zoey's opinion because she would look at it as another artist rather than as a critic. She really wanted Zoey to love it.

'Sure. Let me see.' Zoey stepped out from behind her own easel and came to stand by Erin. 'Oh, wow, that's brilliant!'

Erin felt her heart soar and a broad smile crept across her face. 'You really think so?' It mattered what she thought. It mattered that Zoey loved it.

'Of course! The way you've captured that gentle motion of the sea. The way the sun reflects off the surface.'

'I wasn't sure. I feel it's missing something.'

Zoey stooped to have a closer look, then stood up straight again and gazed out at the sea for some time, before looking back at the painting. 'If it was me, I might add one or two bits of darker contrast up against these lighter parts. Here and maybe here. A dark blue-green. What do you think?'

As soon as she said it, Erin realised that she was right. Sometimes she was afraid to go too dark, but it was exactly what the picture needed to add depth to the water and hint at undercurrents and movement. It was like knowing Zoey. Erin had thought that her life was okay and then Zoey had arrived in it and just knowing her had added an extra element to her life, adding just what she'd needed in that moment.

'You're right. Thank you.'

Zoey smiled at her. 'Want to see mine?'

'Is that okay?'

'Of course! Come look!'

Erin stepped over to look at Zoey's painting. She was capturing Westcombe itself, nestled in the valley between two headlands. A little of the beach. A hint of the sea coming in at one corner of the canvas. Her brushstrokes had been light and free. A hint of being abstract, but with lots of colour. It was a happy picture.

'I love this!'

'You like it? You can have it.'

'Oh, I couldn't possibly take it!'

Zoey reached out then, laid her hand on Erin's arm and looked into her eyes. 'I'd like you to have it. I really would.'

Erin didn't know what to say. She knew what she wanted to do. She wanted to hug her. Maybe drop a kiss onto her soft, sweet lips. Taste her again. But she didn't want to rush things, didn't want to overstep, because Zoey felt like a precipice to Erin. If she allowed herself to do those things, if she threw caution to the wind and forgot all her doubts, she knew, with absolute certainty, that she was going to fall hard for Zoey and fall fast, and if she did that? Then she'd be vulnerable again to being hurt. To having her heart broken, and she didn't dare to rush in, no matter how much she wanted to. Too much was at stake.

'Thank you. And you must have mine. Let's call it an art swap.'

Zoey let go, still smiling, unaware of the turmoil in Erin's soul. 'Perfect. Should we get something to eat? I don't know about you, but I'm starving.'

Erin was hungry. For something more than food. But she could eat. She nodded her agreement and they both unpacked the cooler that Erin had brought and set up their little picnic on the viewing point.

It had been easier when they were painting. They had each had something to focus on rather than each other, but now, with nothing to distract them, Zoey felt like she was on some sort of date with a crush and almost felt tongue-tied. She had to keep taking swallows of her drink as her mouth kept drying out. So far, she'd mentioned how nice the weather was today, how lovely the ham in the sandwich was and how sweet the strawberries. Maybe her conversation was so bad that Erin would see her as boring? She hoped not. She wanted nothing more than to impress Erin and have Erin fall in love with her, but maybe that was just fantasy. A dream. Because reality could never be as wonderful as hopes and dreams, right?

Her phone beeped.

'It's Hazel. Thinks she's having some Braxton Hicks.' These were early, painless practice contractions the body could go through in advance of labour.

Erin nodded. 'Has she thought of any names yet?'

'I think she's always been afraid to. Giving the baby a name makes her a real person and I think she wants to have the baby in her arms, safe and sound, before she names her.'

'Jenna and I used to dream of names we'd call our children.'

'What did you choose?'

Erin shrugged. 'I always had a hankering for Elliot if it was a boy, and Eliana for a girl.'

'Those are beautiful names.'

'Thanks. Funny thing is, Jenna always wanted Finlay for a boy and Jessica for a girl and when she had her little boy with her ex-boyfriend, guess what name she gave him?'

'I want to say Finlay, but from your voice I'm guessing she chose something else?'

'She called him Elliot. Asked if I'd mind. Said she'd slowly fallen in love with the name after all.'

Zoey looked at Erin. 'Did you mind?'

'Of course I did. To begin with. It felt like a taunt. Like she'd named her child with the name I'd wanted for my own son. It almost felt like she was saying, *Hey, Erin, I gave him your name but he'll never be yours.*' Erin shrugged. 'But I got over it.'

'It must have hurt, though.'

'For a little while. Have you heard anything recently from your in-laws?'

'No. It's been radio silence since I ignored Brad's birthday celebration.'

'Does it bother you that their love had conditions?'

'To begin with. But then I realised that if I had to jump through hoops to earn their love, then it was never love to begin with. If you're going to love someone, then do it.'

'Sometimes that's easier said than done.'

Zoey nodded, smiling sadly. She would love to be able to love Erin freely and openly, but it would shock so many people and she was scared of it herself. She'd never been in a long-term relationship with another woman. Would it become comfortable, the way it had with Brad? Would they stop trying to date the other person? Would they stop making an effort if they moved in together, or got married? Once the excitement waned, what would happen between them then? Would the people of Westcombe accept them? Would Hazel? She didn't seem to have a problem with gay people, but that attitude might change once she realised it was her sister. And Hazel needed her so much right now, and in the future, she couldn't afford a falling out with her. Hazel needed her. So did the baby. Without Zoey, that baby would only know its mother for family. Have online video calls with its grandparents, which weren't the same. She'd come here for her fresh start and she was looking forward to becoming an aunt. She couldn't risk losing everything because she followed an impulse and a wild whim.

*Erin's not a whim. I know she's not a whim. I'm using that as an excuse because I'm so scared.*

'Family means everything to me,' she said, pausing before looking back up and at Erin. 'But I'm so glad that I met you. You've already changed my life in so many ways. It's been a long time since I was this happy.'

Erin stared at her. A smile ghosting her face. 'I feel the same way about you, too.'

The words Zoey wanted to say were right there on the tip of her tongue. The urge to say them, to let them just come tumbling out, was so powerful right now, but fear of doing so created a dam. It would be wrong to tell Erin that she was developing strong feelings for her when she could not give Erin what she needed. She'd promised Hazel she'd be there for her. That she'd help out. Committed herself to her family. Her sister. If she told Erin how she really felt, she would then have to tell her that they would need to be a secret and she wasn't sure that Erin would want to live like that. And why should she? She'd never hidden her love before. Would she do so with Zoey? Dare she ask?

But her tongue felt tied and the words stayed resolutely inside.

A seagull landed by their picnic blanket and stalked over to eye the display of food still remaining. It squawked at them both, irritated that they were guarding the food, and Zoey smiled, tossing it a small crumb to appease it.

Was that what she would have to survive on for the next few months? Crumbs of affection from Erin, given in secret. Or could she be bolder? Storm the picnic and take what she wanted for herself? To feed her hunger, her desire for connection with Erin.

Because she craved the feeling of being in

Erin's arms again. Craved the press of her lips against her own.

But duty to her family made her hold back.

*Am I making myself small again? To make everyone else happy.*

# CHAPTER ELEVEN

'THERE WE GO. That's what's been causing all of your problems.' Erin held up the pair of tweezers with a sliver of ingrowing toenail that had been digging in Monty Jessop's big toe for him to see.

Monty stared back at it with a shaking head. 'How can something so small cause so much pain and so many problems?'

Erin smiled. 'I think that's life in a nutshell for you.' She placed the specimen down on the tray and then used gauze to wipe the wound, before using silver nitrate to press down into the nail bed to stop the nail from re-growing there.

'Thank you for removing it.' He sighed, letting out a breath. 'Should be easier to walk now. I've missed doing a lot of the things I love, like walking the coastal paths, for a long time. When can I get back into that?'

'Well, just because the issue has been removed doesn't mean you're healed straight away. I'd take it easy for a few days. Give the toe time to get better and then start small, see how you go.'

'What would I do without you, Dr Bramley? You're my star.'

She smiled and thought about her own star—Zoey. For a moment there, up on that clifftop, when they'd begun talking about love, she'd hoped, briefly, that Zoey might declare her true feelings, only she hadn't. Hope could be a terrible thing, she thought. It could be mean. Teasing. Breathtaking. And then? When hope faded? Awful. Crushing, almost. Erin had returned home from their painting day, their picnic day, feeling frustrated, even though she'd been the one to tell Zoey that they could go slow and here she was, wishing they could just rush into one another's arms!

Instead, she'd just had to sit there, telling herself that everything came to those who wait. That she needed to be patient. This wasn't easy or straightforward for Zoey. It was for Erin because she had always been open about her sexuality. But Zoey hadn't. She'd been married to a guy for fifteen years! And if her family had no idea then that could come as a bit of a shock, and Erin knew that Zoey loved her family and her sister in particular. A sister that she had moved to Westcombe to be with!

Coming out wasn't always easy, the way it had been for her. Erin's coming out had been no surprise to anyone. There'd never been any posters of male pop stars or actors on her walls growing up, only women. She'd never had a boyfriend at school, only girlfriends that came around. Whenever she drew or painted as a teenager, it had always been of women. Their hands. Eyes. Lips. It had seemed so easy to one day sit down with her mum and tell her that she had a crush on this girl called Jenna. It had never been an issue for her and just because it had never been an issue for her, she had to make herself remember that it would not be that easy for everyone else to come out to their family. The world was more accepting these days, but it still wasn't perfect and there were still problems for some.

She finished dressing Monty's toe, said goodbye and left the procedure room to consult on who was next. A Warren Smith who was due a freezing treatment on a wart on his back.

Erin sighed. If only love could be dealt with so easily with a quick blast of liquid nitrogen.

*Freeze my heart to stop it from hurting so much.*

It was the end of another long day and Zoey felt exhausted. She'd had three patients today that had gone over their allotted time; because their emotions had been so overwhelming she'd needed to take extra time with them. Sara Petworth had cried with anxiety during her consult and Zoey was not so cold-hearted that she could just let her go in that state and so she'd sat with her and discussed what was bothering her for a lot longer than the ten minutes most consults were meant to take. Then there'd been Edgar Dooley, who'd just lost his daughter to motor neurone disease, and she had never seen a man so broken by loss and so she'd sat with him and listened and offered advice, and she'd only let him go once he was more himself again. And lastly there'd been a woman so harangued by her husband because he didn't like the changes that had swept over his wife from menopause. Her clinic had overrun so late she was surprised that she wasn't the only one left in the building.

Erin was still in her consulting room, typing up notes still from her procedure clinic day.

'Hey. Thought I was the only one left.'

Erin looked up from the glow of her computer screen with a smile. 'Oh, you know how it is. The procedures are quick, but the paperwork is endless.'

'Preach. You look tired.'

'Thanks, I think.'

Zoey closed the door behind her. She didn't know what it was that compelled her—maybe it was all the emotional range that she had witnessed and felt today but she needed a hug more than anything. She walked over to Erin's chair, spun her around to face her and made her stand, before sinking into her embrace and just being held.

Zoey closed her eyes in bliss.

This was what she had been craving. This moment of peace. This moment that was just for her and Erin. Their bodies fitted together so perfectly.

Brad had never really been a hugger. Neither had her parents. So what was it about the simple need to be held? Acceptance? Love? A moment of stillness. Of recognition. That the other person needed something in that moment that only a pair of loving arms could provide. It almost felt like their heartbeats were syncing…

Erin smelt like antiseptic and soap, but she felt like home.

'You okay?' Erin asked softly.

'Mm-hmm. Is this okay?'

'Of course.'

She could feel Erin's soft touch. A gentle stroke of her hair. A smoothing of her back. A warmth. A feeling of belonging. She never wanted it to end, but her mobile phone began to ring with Hazel's ringtone and though Zoey yearned to ignore it and just enjoy this moment for a little bit longer, duty pulled her from Erin's embrace.

'I'd better get that.'

Erin nodded.

Rummaging in her bag, she finally pulled out the irritating phone. 'Hey. Everything okay?'

'My waters broke this afternoon and I'm in labour. I'm at the hospital. Please tell me you're already at home and you can make it here!' Hazel's pleading, frightened voice came over the phone.

'I'll be right there.'

She saw Erin frown with concern. 'What's happening?'

Zoey stared at Erin, their moment forgotten. 'Hazel's gone into labour. She's at the hospital.'

'She's early,' Erin said. 'Let me drive you.'

'It's okay. I can go by myself.'

'You're worried. Let me drive you, then I'll know that you'll have got there in one piece.'

'You're sure?'

Erin softened and reached up to stroke Zoey's face. 'Of course I'm sure.'

'Thank you.' She wanted to melt into Erin's touch, but she couldn't. Already, concern for Hazel and her baby was the overriding emotion in that moment. She would have to make sure that Erin kept her distance at the hospital. She'd hate for the drama of the moment to cause them to give themselves away to her sister. She would tell Hazel one day, but not today. Not tomorrow. Would she ever? The idea so terrified her she almost couldn't think straight.

As they drove to West General Hospital, she

hoped that her sister was okay. Should she phone her parents? Let them know what was happening? *No, I don't want to worry them that the baby's coming early.* Hazel was thirty-seven weeks, so the baby would most probably be fine at this gestation, but you never could tell what would happen during labour and delivery and until that baby was safely in her sister's arms, Zoey wasn't sure she'd be able to relax.

*I'm about to be an aunt!*

Parking was horrendous, so Erin dropped Zoey off at Maternity and said she'd find them later.

Zoey hurried into the department, passed the ultrasound department and went up to Labour and Delivery, which was on the first floor. She pressed the door buzzer.

'Hello?'

'Hi. I'm Hazel Wilson's sister. I'm her birth partner; I got told she's been admitted.'

The door buzzed open and she pushed her way through and hurried up to Reception. 'Hazel Wilson?'

The kind-faced receptionist pointed down the hallway. 'Room four.'

'Thanks.'

She hoped everything was going fine. First deliveries could take a while, but they were also nerve-racking because you had no idea how this person would deal with labour or how the baby would be. Zoey forced away the memory of one of her patients who went into labour thinking everything was fine, only for her baby to be stillborn. Sometimes she hated being a doctor because she knew of all the things that could go wrong and she'd often met the people that it happened to.

She rapped her knuckles on the door to Room four.

'Come in!' said a voice.

Zoey popped her head around the door and saw her sister lying on a bed, strapped to a CTG machine that was tracking her contractions and monitoring baby's heartbeat. A reassuring rhythmic sound filled the room.

Hazel visibly relaxed at seeing Zoey there. 'You made it! Thank God!'

'Nothing was going to keep me away from this!' Zoey said, smiling, entering the room and swooping down to press a kiss on her sister's cheek. 'How are you doing?'

'Not bad. Happier now I'm here and in closer proximity to drugs.' Hazel smiled.

'And baby's happy at the moment. I'm Marie, Hazel's designated midwife.' Marie reached out her hand for Zoey to shake.

'Zoey. Sister.'

'She's a doctor,' Hazel told Marie.

'Oh, okay. What kind?'

'General practice,' Zoey said, hanging her bag around the back of the seat next to her sister's bed.

'How do you like that? Are the hours good?'

'They can be long, but thankfully no night shifts like you guys.'

Marie smiled and turned back to the trace. 'Well, Hazel, everything looks great right now. We'll keep you on this for about another ten minutes and then, if there's no worries, we'll get you off it and you can start moving around. Have you got a preference regarding pain relief?'

'I'd like an epidural if possible.'

'I'll let the anaesthetist know when they're free. They're currently in Theatre, but it's not pressing yet because you seem to be coping okay. Can I get you anything, Zoey? A tea? Coffee? Water?'

'Oh, I'm fine, thank you.'

'No worries.' Marie disappeared from the room.

Zoey turned back to her sister. 'She seems nice.'

'She is.'

'So, this is it, huh?'

Hazel nodded. 'No turning back now. Should I call him?' She meant the father of the baby.

'That's up to you.'

'He's not wanted anything to do with the pregnancy. I think I'm too emotional right now to hear he's not going to show up for the labour either.'

'Want me to call him?'

'Would you? This is his number. I just think he should know it's happening, at least.'

'I'll go out and call him. I won't be long, okay?' She could see how stressed Hazel was. The moment she'd been waiting for, the moment she'd feared, was finally here and she would do whatever her sister needed to help her get through it.

Hazel nodded and smiled, smoothing her hand over her swollen belly as another contraction began to build.

Zoey stayed with her through it. Marie was right. Hazel was coping well with them. The trace seemed to indicate that her contractions were about forty to forty-five seconds long and happening every few minutes. This could be fast, so she didn't want to linger too long outside on a phone call with the errant father.

She kissed Zoey's cheek and headed into the corridor.

Erin felt as if she'd waited an age for a parking space and once she'd bought a ticket for a couple of hours she headed inside to the maternity unit. As soon as she walked through the doors, her own mobile went and she pulled it from her pocket and gazed at the screen in shock.

Jenna was calling her.

What could she possibly want? And after all this time. Erin had moved on. Built a new life. Worked damned hard to try and forget the woman who had broken her heart—and now she was calling? Like a ghost from her past.

*It could be about Elliot.*

Frowning, not really wanting to answer, she pressed accept and lifted the phone to her ear.

'Erin?'

Hearing her voice again sent shivers down Erin's spine. It was as if all the time she'd spent apart from this woman disappeared in an instant.

'What do *you* want, Jenna?'

Jenna gave a small, awkward laugh. 'I, er…well…to be honest with you… I wondered if maybe we could meet up?'

'Why?' She could comprehend of no reason for it.

'I broke up with him. Things weren't working out for us. We weren't compatible. We realised we were only together for the sake of Elliot, so…yeah. I thought maybe…*we* could give it another go?'

Erin stopped walking towards Maternity. There were security doors there and she stood in a small atrium with plenty of seats. Clearly, people waited out here a lot. But she didn't want to sit. She needed to pace.

'You are joking?'

'No, I'm not.' Jenna sounded earnest. Desperate. 'I made a mistake, okay? I made a stupid, terrible mistake! But we could both have what we've always dreamed of! A family together! You, me and Elliot. Isn't that what you've always wanted?'

Erin gave a sardonic laugh. Of course that was what she'd wanted. Once upon a time when she'd thought she was important to Jenna. 'You think you can just call me up and think that I'll come back to you after what you did?'

'Of course not. We'd need to talk, but… I think we could really be happy together if we tried.'

'Yeah, well, I don't need to try, because I have someone else in my life right now. Something that doesn't seem to have occurred to you. And do you know the difference between you and her?'

There was no answer.

'The difference is that she respects the fact that she holds my heart in her hands. She is careful with it. Gentle. Kind. Loving. And the idea that she might hurt me is abhorrent to her!'

'Do I know her?'

'No. It's no one you know.'

'So, you've moved on?'

'I have.'

'Can she offer you a family? A child?'

Erin was incredulous. 'Are you trying to use Elliot as some kind of guilt-inducing bargaining chip? Wow! I really never knew you at all, did I?'

'Are you and her serious?'

Erin almost couldn't believe she was still talking to her. All this time she'd spent mourning the loss of her ex and it turned out there'd never been a reason for it. Because Jenna was not someone she could ever imagine being back with.

'That's none of your business.'

'You're going to throw away everything we could possibly have—a future, a family—over someone who you're not sure of?'

'I never threw anything away and I never said I wasn't sure about Zoey.'

'Zoey?' A pause. 'Pretty name. Just…promise me that you won't rush into anything. That you'll consider what I've said. Don't you want a family?'

'Of course I do, Jenna. You know I do. But I think—no, I know—I've found it elsewhere.' She heard her voice break on the words.

'Please don't give up on us, Erin. I've missed you so much.'

'I've missed you, too.' *But the version I've missed was never really real, was she?*

'Will you call me later?'

Erin wanted to say no. But it seemed so abrupt and rude. 'I don't think so.'

'Please, Erin!'

Erin ended the call. There was no point in it continuing. Jenna had shown her true colours and now found herself in a situation where she was the one left wanting and pining for what they'd once had. But Erin had been through that mire and she never wanted to go back.

She turned around to head to the double doors, to get access to Maternity and join Zoey and Hazel. She pressed the buzzer for admission.

Zoey had just finished her phone call with Jeremy, the father of Hazel's baby, and it hadn't gone well. Hazel had been left well and truly alone, without support from the dad.

*Poor Hazel!*

And there was only one thing she could do to make that message from him not be so upsetting and that was to be there for her, no matter what. She would not let her sister down! Would not abandon her and would soften the message as much as she could when she went back into the room.

At the end of the corridor, the doors swung open and there was Erin. Lovely, wonderful Erin. Her face full of joy at seeing her.

And in that moment the world froze as she realised she would have to make a decision.

Hazel or Erin?

She loved them both, but Hazel needed her now more than ever and anything with Erin would have to be put to one side, because Hazel didn't know about her attraction to women and she wasn't brave enough to tell her. Hazel's emotions and hormones would be all over the place right now and she could react badly to the news, and honestly? Zoey wasn't sure she could stand losing Hazel too. In the last two years, she'd lost a husband, a job, a home, a family. And even though some of those things had felt more like millstones around her neck, she'd had a support network and she'd come here to Westcombe to support her sister and that was who was important right now and she refused to let her down in this, the most important moment of her life.

Could she risk it all on what could be a mirage? Just like it had been with Violet? Fooling herself that the relationship could be something more.

She'd been a terrible fool to believe it had been anything else. Well, there was no time for her to worry about all of that now. Hazel was what was important. Hazel and her baby. Family. Family was the most important thing.

'Can I help you?' a midwife called out to Erin.

'Oh, I'm with them,' she said, pointing at Zoey.

'Are you family?'

Erin hesitated. 'Er…no, but—'

'You should go home,' Zoey said to Erin, hating the words as they spilled from her mouth, but she had to do the right thing by her sister and make her the priority.

'What?'

'It's family only and um…' She could feel her heart breaking with every syllable. Could feel the words choking in her throat, not wanting to be said, but saying them anyway, because this came down to a choice and she could only choose her sister right now. 'I'm choosing Hazel right now. Her. Not you.'

Erin stared at her.

'Thank you for the lift.' And she escaped into her sister's room, fighting back tears, fighting the urge to scream and shout and hate herself for hurting Erin, but she'd had to do it! She couldn't lose her sister! She needed her!

'Oh, God, what did he say?' Hazel asked, no doubt seeing the upset on her face.

Of course. Yes. She still had to deliver that unappealing bit of news. Zoey had to think back. To rewind. To gather herself and be strong for Hazel.

'He said no. I'm so sorry. He just wasn't interested, but he did say that he wished you the best.' The father of Hazel's baby hadn't even been that kind. They were words that Zoey had come up with to soften the blow.

Hazel's face fell. 'What about when she's born? Doesn't he want to know?'

*'I told her to get rid of it! What do I care?'* His cruel words still reverberated in her head, but she would never tell them to Hazel.

Zoey shook her head and reached for Hazel's hand, needing the touch more than Hazel probably did. Then, as Hazel was gathering herself, Zoey realised something. The sound of the baby's heartbeat was different from before. It was slower. She let go of her sister's hand and went to look at the trace. There'd been one or two decelerations before, but baby had recovered its rhythm, but right now? The heart rate had decreased and stayed low. This wasn't good.

'I need to fetch Marie.'

'Why? What's wrong? Ooh…' Another contraction began, but Zoey couldn't waste any time explaining. She ran from the room and called the midwife's name. A quick glance up and down the corridor told her that Erin had gone. Marie was just coming out of another room, sliding her pen into her scrubs top pocket.

'Zoey? Something wrong?'

'Baby's bradycardic. Heart trace has decelerated and stayed low since her last contraction.'

'Okay, let me take a look.' Marie headed into Hazel's room.

Erin stood staring at the door to labour room number four. She felt numb. In shock. Reeling from the sudden reappearance of Jenna into her life and her wicked attempt to manipulate her into taking her back, and then for Zoey—dear, darling Zoey—to block her out!

*'Not you.'*

*Not you!*

She had no words. How had everything changed so quickly? Zoey had hugged her at the surgery! Sank into her arms and she'd felt so good and her hair had smelled so heavenly and Erin had fought the urge to let her hands wander and explore more, because she'd known, in that moment, that all Zoey needed was a hug. Some recognition. Some affection after a hard day. And she'd given her that. Gladly. Happily enjoying the unexpected contact from the woman that she had come to love.

It had surprised her, that love.

The suddenness of it. The impulsivity of it. How quickly it had grown in so short a time. But, she'd told herself, when it was the right person, perhaps it did happen that quickly. Maybe that was why she had tried to fight it for so long. Why she'd suggested that they go slow, because *she'd* been the one who'd needed to accept her feelings for Zoey.

What had changed?

Maybe it was the intensity of the moment? The impending birth?

*Or she's embarrassed about us. Too afraid to let her sister, or the world, know about what we have?*

Zoey had made a choice and Erin was being *rejected.* Not good enough. Again. Zoey wanted family and clearly wanted to build that with Hazel and the baby. The way Jenna had wanted to build a family with her ex and Elliot.

*I'm not enough for anyone!*

She wondered if there was any point in fighting this. Was she just going to give up? Without protest. Was there any point in holding on? On holding onto hope that Zoey would eventually be brave enough to tell everyone about them?

*No. Because if I can be discarded so quickly and so easily by someone, then it was never love for them and I've had a lucky escape.*

*If she loved me, then she wouldn't want to keep things quiet. She'd want to tell the whole world! Like I wanted to.*

She knew she'd been right to reject Jenna.

But couldn't bear the fact that she'd been wrong about Zoey.

* * *

‘We’re going to need to take you into Theatre.’

The lead doctor had arrived. Lots of important and busy people had arrived in Hazel’s room after Marie had looked at the trace.

Baby was in distress for some reason and her heart rate wasn’t recovering or dealing well with the contractions. It could be for any number of reasons. Reasons they wouldn’t or couldn’t know until they went in via Caesarean section.

Hazel nodded, looking pale and frightened. ‘Can my sister come in with me?’

‘I’m afraid not. It’s going to be a general anaesthetic.’

Zoey stepped forward to take her sister’s hand as the medical staff began unplugging her bed and getting ready to move her quickly. ‘I’ll be right outside though. You can do this!’

‘What about the baby?’

‘She’s in good hands. We’re going to be okay.’

Hazel nodded, but then she was gone and the room was empty and Zoey was left standing on her own.

There had been times in her life where she’d felt alone before. In her marriage to Brad. After being used by Violet. Most visits to her in-laws’ house, where she’d felt more of an accessory than a real person of importance. After Brad’s funeral. Most nights in the house they'd bought together.

But now she felt truly alone. Not even Erin to hold her hand and just be there for her. *Imagine if she was by my side right now? If I'd been courageous enough.*

A solitary tear ran down her cheek.

Sadness or fear? Or both? She felt sure Hazel would be okay, but what would happen to them all if something happened to this baby? Hazel was scared of being a mother, but imagine how she'd feel if she was a mother to a baby that didn't survive birth? Carrying it for all those months. Suffering the nausea she had all the way through the pregnancy. Only to lose it at the last hurdle.

The room seemed so empty and quiet.

She could hear a newborn baby crying down the corridor. The sound of a new mother trying to soothe that baby.

Should she pray? Did she believe in a God that had taken away anyone she'd ever cared about? Violet. Brad. Her parents. Was Hazel next? Was the baby?

*I don't even want to think about Erin.*

There was so much risk in allowing yourself to love someone. And maybe if everything went all right, then she would allow herself to grieve about Erin when she got home, but right now? She couldn't.

Her heart was with her sister.

And whatever was happening in Theatre.

# CHAPTER TWELVE

'HI! I'M HOME!' Zoey closed the front door of the cottage behind her, hung up her bag and followed the sound of baby Sienna crying.

Hazel was in the living room, which had somehow turned into baby central, holding her crying daughter, swaying her, trying her hardest to get her to stop crying. But it also looked like Hazel had been crying too. Her eyes were red and swollen. 'She's been like this for over an hour! Do you think something's wrong?'

Zoey could hear the distress in her voice. Sienna was a vocal baby with a good pair of lungs on her. After a long day at work, covering for Erin, who had taken some time off and hadn't been seen since the hospital, she wasn't sure she had the energy for soothing either of them, but she was willing to give it a go.

'Let me take her. She probably senses that you're upset and so is she. Why don't you go take a shower?'

Sienna's face was red and puffy from crying

too and Zoey could feel the rigid tension in the little girl's body.

'Are you sure?' Hazel asked.

'Of course. You go. When did she last have a feed?'

'Ten minutes ago.'

Zoey nodded. Okay, so she didn't have to worry about feeding her. 'Just go and take a shower.'

'You're a lifesaver.' Hazel gave her a grateful smile that said so much.

When she was gone, Zoey looked down at her niece and gently soothed her, singing the lullabies she remembered her own mother singing to her.

It was lovely to have a baby in the house. Was this what she'd been missing all these years? Was this what Brad had dreamed would fix them? What Serena and Geoffrey longed for? Sienna was sweet. Even when she was upset.

But it would be nice to be able to share her with someone. She'd once imagined that Erin would be that someone. That they could babysit together on occasion. Erin would have loved that. Zoey knew how much Erin had wanted to be a mother.

And now Erin was gone. *Have I hurt her? Did I ruin us both?*

Now that they were home from the hospital,

away from the drama and tension of Sienna's delivery—her heart rate had decelerated because she'd had loops of umbilical cord around her neck—she was able to think more clearly than she had all week. She'd tried calling Erin, but she wasn't answering. She'd even knocked on her door to see if they could talk frankly and get everything into the open. Because she needed to be sure. Needed to know for definite if she'd ruined her own future happiness or not. Because even though she loved Hazel and Sienna, she'd realised that she'd prioritized everyone else's happiness before her own once again. Something she'd sworn she would never do again. Yes, she'd come to Westcombe to be there for her sister as she became a mother, but she'd also come here for the freedom to find out who she was.

At work it was strange. They'd called in an agency locum GP and it was weird to see a different face in Erin's room. Sometimes she'd almost forget, go to rap her knuckles against the wood and ask if she wanted to join her for lunch, and then she'd remember.

The pain.

The loss.

The solitariness of moving through life without Erin there. These last few days had been emotionally, mentally and physically exhausting. Working all day and then coming home and helping Hazel mind the baby.

Sienna was settling. Clearly affected by Zoey's calmer mood and soothing murmurs.

Zoey was walking her up and down, up and down, talking to her softly as she did so about anything that came to mind. Her art now up on the walls. Erin's painting of the sea. Water that looked calm and pretty, but had dangerous undertows and currents that couldn't be seen. What her Auntie Zoey had been up to today. The pretty birds in the garden.

'That was amazing. Thanks for that. Auntie Zoey clearly has that magical touch,' Hazel said, returning from her shower, wet hair wrapped up in a towel, scooping her daughter from Zoey's arms and placing her down in her Moses basket.

'Hazel, I…'

Her sister turned to look at her, her face expectant. 'What's up?'

Could she tell her? *Should* she? Risk telling her sister her biggest secret, when Hazel still needed assistance? What if it ruined their relationship, when the relationship she'd had with Erin was over anyway? What was the point?

But the truth of it inside of her was eating her up and if she didn't get it out, it might consume her.

'I… I have something to tell you.'

'Okay. What is it?'

'Would you sit down?'

Hazel perched on the arm of the sofa. 'Sitting. What is it? You're scaring me a little.' She suddenly jumped back up. 'Is something wrong with Sienna?'

'No, no!' Zoey shook her head and guided her sister back over to the couch and sat with her and impulsively reached for her hands and held them, feeling her pulse thrum in her ears and her mouth went dry.

'It's about me.'

'Okaaaay?'

Where to start? How to start?

'Is this about Erin?' Hazel asked.

Zoey blushed instantly. 'Why do you ask that?'

'Because we haven't seen her since she brought you to the hospital? Because she's your next-door neighbour and she strikes me as the kind of nice person who might bring flowers or a gift for the baby and she hasn't come around? Did you two have a falling out or something?'

'A bit.'

'I thought so. You two should make up.'

Zoey almost cried. 'I'd love to, but… I don't know where she is!'

'I saw her in the back garden earlier, when I was trying to settle Sienna.'

'You saw her? She's back?'

Hazel nodded, smiling. 'It's okay, you know.'

'What is?' Her mind was reeling. Erin was back? She couldn't concentrate on what Hazel was saying.

'You two. Together. It's cute!'

'*Wait—what?*' Hazel *knew*?

'Sis, I was pregnant, not blind. What happened to you two?'

'You know that I…also like girls?'

'Sweetie, I've known for a long time.'

'But you've never said anything!' This was a shock.

'I figured you'd tell me in your own time, but honestly? Sometimes? You're so bloody self-sacrificing! Look at how long you stayed with Brad because it was easier than telling people what you really wanted! If you could stand that, I figured it wasn't my place to rock the boat, but living with you this past week? You've been great and I could not have done this without you, but you cannot do this without *her*! You love her, don't you?'

A solitary tear dripped down Zoey's cheek. 'Yes.'

'Then go see her. Tell her you're sorry and that you made a mistake.'

'I'm not sure it's going to be that easy.'

'Nothing worth having in life ever is, but if

you love her, truly love her and want to be with her, then you fight for her.'

Zoey couldn't believe it! She'd possibly ruined the greatest love in her life for no reason at all! Because Hazel had known and not said a thing! Maybe communication was something they all needed to work on? Going forward, they could work on that. Being honest. Choosing honesty.

Choosing to be brave.

Choosing to risk rocking the boat.

'What if she doesn't want me back?'

'Then you'll have to respect that, but talk to her, Zo! Tell her you were scared. I'll bet you'll find that she was, too.'

'I love you.' Zoey threw her arms around her sister and gave her a hug.

Hazel laughed. 'Now go tell Erin the same thing. It's amazing what power a declaration of love can hold.'

Erin was sitting in her back garden and she was trying to paint the flowers in her flowerbed. The canvas was filled with a cacophony of colour and blooms and Erin was staring at it with a frown.

'You're home...' Zoey said, a moment or two after she'd spent a few seconds soaking in the sight of her. She'd missed her. Terribly so.

Erin leapt to her feet, startled. Clearly, she'd not heard Zoey's approach. 'I never left.'

'I thought you'd gone away. I haven't seen you. I tried calling, but you never answered.'

'I was hiding.' Erin shrugged. 'Licking my wounds.'

Zoey had caused those wounds. 'I'm sorry.'

'I've heard the baby. Is she all right?'

Zoey nodded. 'She's fine. Got a good pair of lungs on her.'

'I've heard her. What's her name?'

'Sienna.'

Erin smiled. 'That's pretty.'

'I see you're painting. It looks great.'

Erin bent to pick it up and look at it, shrugging. 'It's at the messy stage. Things have to get messy before they can become beautiful.'

Zoey thought Erin was beautiful. Seeing her again like this, after being parted for nearly a whole week, was agony! 'I've missed you.'

'Have you?' Erin didn't seem so sure about that.

'Yes. Incredibly so. Did you…miss me?'

'More than my heart could bear.'

That gave her a little hope. Maybe Erin could forgive her?

'I'm sorry about what I said in the hospital. I panicked. Thought I had to make a choice. I thought choosing Hazel and the baby would be enough for me. To stay safe. To stop myself from losing her too. It was a knee-jerk reaction and

I can't apologise enough for how I behaved so abruptly and for what I said to you.'

'I did wonder what had happened to make you push me away like that.'

'Can you forgive me?'

Erin looked at her then, with such love in her eyes, with such pain still, that it almost broke Zoey's heart to see it.

'I love you, Zoey. I didn't understand what had happened and yes, I hid away, because I needed to work out in my own mind what I felt. What I wanted to feel. Being away from you has been a torture, knowing you were just next door. Seeing your name pop up on my phone. But I needed to understand and now you've told me. If you need space, I will give it to you, but I'd like to think that we could be something.'

'You love me?' Zoey couldn't hide her joy at hearing those words. 'You really mean it?' Could it be possible that happiness could come from such a disaster?

'Believe me, I've tried not to.' Erin came to stand in front of her and reached for her hand to hold in her own.

'Love has never worked out for me, Erin, and I just assumed it wouldn't again. But to hear you say you love me...' She beamed. 'You should know that...well, I love you, too.'

Erin smiled and pulled her in close and their

lips met in the most exquisite kiss that Zoey had ever had in her entire life. One filled with love and wonder and beauty. With fire and passion. With heat. There was intent in that kiss.

A promise.

For a better future.

'Well, about bloody time!' said Hazel's voice from behind the fence.

They broke apart, Zoey gasping, laughing, that her sister had overheard. 'Hazel?'

Her sister's head popped up from behind the fence. She must have been standing on an overturned flowerpot or something. 'Hello. Erin. Good to see you again.'

'Hazel! Congratulations on the baby.'

'Thank you. Can you promise to look after my sister and never hurt her? She's been through a lot.'

'I can promise to try.'

'That's good enough for me. Oh, I can hear my daughter waking up. Better go get her before the whole of Westcombe complains about her.' She gave them both a wink and stepped down and away. They heard the back door close as she went inside.

Zoey turned back to Erin. Everything was going to be fine! She wasn't losing anyone!

Erin pulled her back into an embrace. 'Now

then…where were we before we got rudely interrupted?'

Zoey smiled. 'I think you were kissing me.'

'And you were kissing me. Want to go for round two?'

'As long as it never ends.' Zoey pulled her in for another kiss.

Summer had never tasted so good.

# EPILOGUE

PLANNING PERMISSION TO knock the two cottages together had passed easily and the work had been completed just a few months ago. It had taken some time for them to repaint and redecorate, but now Seaglass Cottage was looking wonderful and, better than that, they'd been able to dedicate one of the bedrooms to an artists' studio where they both could paint. Erin had even managed to sell a couple of pieces and the art gallery in Westcombe had let them both have a wall to display their pieces.

Erin and Zoey were happier than they could ever have imagined and their relationship was going from strength to strength. Now they were celebrating Sienna's first birthday and the cottage was filled with mums and friends and Zoey's parents had flown in from Australia to meet their granddaughter for the first time.

It was hectic and noisy, but perfect. Erin had never believed that she could feel so fulfilled, but she did. She was Auntie Erin to Sienna and there was nothing that she and Zoey liked better than to babysit their beautiful little niece.

As the party continued in the cottage, Erin took a moment to find Zoey and extricate her from a couple who were monopolizing her attention and took her hand to lead her out into the garden.

The summer was another hot one and the garden looked amazing at this time of year. She led Zoey down a small garden path that took them all the way to the back, because for this next part of their lives, she wanted them to have privacy. For it to be just them.

'Where are we going?' Zoey asked, laughing, a flute of champagne in her other hand.

'I want to show you something.'

'Have you bought that water feature you've been going on about?'

'No. There's a rock I want to show you.'

'A rock?' Zoey sounded unsure. Puzzled.

But when they reached the trellis arch, adorned with jasmine and a pink climbing rose, Erin stopped and turned to face her and just briefly, for a moment, she stared into Zoey's eyes and felt scared. She might say no, but she doubted it. She and Zoey had been incredibly happy since they'd become an official couple.

'There's something I've been meaning to ask you for a very long time.'

'Okaaay.'

Erin took hold of Zoey's champagne flute and placed it on the ground, then she reached into her own pocket and pulled out the small red velvet box shaped like a heart and opened it, to reveal a beautiful diamond solitaire ring that glinted and gleamed in the hot summer sun.

'This rock. You have made me so very happy and I've never felt more fulfilled than when I've been with you. And I'd like that to be permanent. I'd like for us to be married and so…' Erin sucked in a deep breath. 'I love you with all my heart and my soul, Zoey Alexandra Marsh. Will you marry me?'

Zoey gasped.

Then nodded.

Then burst into tears and laugh cried as Erin slid the ring onto Zoey's finger.

It fitted perfectly.

As if it had always been meant to be.

They kissed. They hugged.

They stopped so Zoey could gaze at the ring in shock again for a moment, then they kissed some more.

Erin knew that they were both going to get their happy ever after.

It had been a long time coming.

But the best things came to those who waited.

* * * * *

*If you enjoyed this story, check out these other great reads from Louisa Heaton*

Onboard and Off Limits
Nurse's Night Before Valentine's
New Year to Nine-Month Surprise
One Night to Twin Miracle

*All available now!*